Acting Edition

The Plot, Like Gravy, Thickens

by Billy St. John

SAMUEL FRENCH

FOR PRODUCTION INQUIRIES

UNITED STATES AND CANADA
info@concordtheatricals.com
1-866-979-0447

UNITED KINGDOM AND EUROPE
licensing@concordtheatricals.co.uk
020-7054-7298

Each title is subject to availability from Concord Theatricals Corp., depending upon country of performance. Please be aware that *THE PLOT, LIKE GRAVY, THICKENS* may not be licensed by Concord Theatricals Corp. in your territory. Professional and amateur producers should contact the nearest Concord Theatricals Corp. office or licensing partner to verify availability.

This work is published by Samuel French, an imprint of Concord Theatricals Corp.

No one shall make any changes in this title(s) for the purpose of production. No part of this book may be reproduced, stored in a retrieval system, scanned, uploaded, or transmitted in any form, by any means, now known or yet to be invented, including mechanical, electronic, digital, photocopying, recording, videotaping, or otherwise, without the prior written permission of the publisher. No one shall share this title(s), or any part of this title(s), through any social media or file hosting websites.

For all inquiries regarding motion picture, television, online/digital and other media rights, please contact Concord Theatricals Corp.

MUSIC AND THIRD-PARTY MATERIALS USE NOTE

Licensees are solely responsible for obtaining formal written permission from copyright owners to use copyrighted music and/or other copyrighted third-party materials (e.g. artworks, logos) in the performance of this play and are strongly cautioned to do so. If no such permission is obtained by the licensee, then the licensee must use only original music and materials that the licensee owns and controls. Licensees are solely responsible and liable for clearances of all third-party copyrighted materials, including without limitation music, and shall indemnify the copyright owners of the play(s) and their licensing agent, Concord Theatricals Corp., against any costs, expenses, losses and liabilities arising from the use of such copyrighted third-party materials by licensees. For music, please contact the appropriate music licensing authority in your territory for the rights to any incidental music.

IMPORTANT BILLING AND CREDIT REQUIREMENTS

If you have obtained performance rights to this title, please refer to your licensing agreement for important billing and credit requirements.

CAST OF CHARACTERS

WALTER: A playwright's alter-ego
who plays the following two characters:
EDWARD WORTHINGTON III : a millionaire, tyrannical, 50
LT. JAMES McMILLAN: a police detective, 30's

ALLEGRA BLACKWELL WORTHINGTON: Edward's attractive
    wife, early 40's
TONY BLACKWELL: Edward's brother-in-law, a playboy, early 30's
JUSTINE WORTHINGTON: Edward's ex-wife, bitter, late 40's
DEBRA WORTHINGTON: Edward's and Justine's daughter, a
    student, 20's
BEATRICE WORTHINGTON: Edward's older sister, a spinster, 60's
ROY PHILLIPS: Edward's business manager, nervous, up-tight, 40's
CONNIE PHILLIPS: Roy's wife, giddy, 30's
PEGGY SUE BRUMLEY: Edward's secretary, a Southern belle, 20's
LAWRENCE TATE: Edward's lawyer, businesslike, 50's
HOLLISTER: the butler, formal, 60's
MRS. VICKERS: the housekeeper, outspoken, 40's
EDITH: the maid, pretty, innocent, 20's
INA: the cook, has a temper, 40's

TIME: The present.
PLACE: The living room of Worthington Manor.

PROLOGUE

ACT I:
A stormy September night.
Scene 1 - About 7:00 o'clock.
Scene 2 - About two hours later.

ACT II:
Several hours later.

PROLOGUE

(The setting is the living room of Worthington Manor, the home of millionaire Edward Worthington III. There is a set of French doors SR that open out to a patio. Its panes are covered with sheers that become transparent when lighted from behind. A backdrop beyond the doors depicts a wide lawn with trees in the distance. An archway with a set of sliding doors is UC. A bell cord hangs SL of the archway, beside a light switch there. When the doors are open, the base of an elegant staircase is seen beyond the arch. A passageway between the stairs and the living room wall leads to the kitchen area and a half-bath. Off UR is an unseen front door that is used for sound effects. This area beyond the archway can be elevated a step on a low platform. A fireplace is on the SL wall. A door above it opens out to a parlor. A round table and four chairs are SR. There is a nice cloth on it, and a small dish of mints. A high-back chair, floor lamp, and end table are against the UR wall to the right of the archway. To the left of the archway, against the UL wall, is a long table. A sofa facing out is SL. A bench is DL of it, before the fireplace. A low-back chair is opposite the bench, DR of the sofa. A coffee table sits below the sofa. The furnishings are elegant, reflecting the home owner's immense wealth. The lighting causes the upper walls to recede into shadows, creating a moody atmosphere.

AT RISE: A storm rages outside. Rain pounds down as lightning flashes and thunder booms beyond the French doors. ALLEGRA stands UC. TONY stands by the fireplace holding a cup of coffee. ALLEGRA wears a beautiful gown; TONY has on a tuxedo. We'll meet them a little later. We have discovered them in the middle of a scene.)

ALLEGRA. Forget about the girl. We've got bigger worries.

TONY. Such as?

ALLEGRA. *(Crossing to UR.)* That document or whatever it is Edward is carrying around.

TONY. What about it?

ALLEGRA. *(Turning back to him.)* It could be our eviction notice.

TONY. What do you mean?

ALLEGRA. I mean, they could be divorce papers. If I'm left out in the cold, you would be too, Tony. We'd both be penniless.

TONY. *(Putting his cup on the mantle.)* Divorce? Are things that bad between you?

ALLEGRA. Edward has grown tired of me, and I suspect he's already picked my replacement. At first I thought he was simply having a mild flirtation with that Dixie Creme donut, Peggy Sue. Now I'm not so sure.

TONY. Peggy Sue? *(Crossing to her.)* She's a knockout, but you're more sophisticated than she is, more glamorous than she is ....

ALLEGRA. *(Cutting in.)* Twenty years older than she is. That hominy-fed hussy has one thing I don't, Tony — youth — and that's one thing Edward's money can't buy me.

TONY. Edward's money — it should be your money, too! If he hadn't made you sign that agreement ....

ALLEGRA. But he did. I'm afraid the only way his fortune could possibly become mine is if he were to drop dead before he divorced me.

(WALTER can be sitting on a step to the audience watching from the beginning of the scene, or he can enter DL from the wings. He holds a legal pad on which he's been writing, and a pen.)

WALTER. Okay, hold it..... *(TONY and ALLEGRA stop and turn to face him. Whenever WALTER talks to the audience, all of the actors will relax and look at him with basically blank expressions until they respond to him, talk to the audience, or go back into character to play a scene.)* That looked pretty good. *(Calling out.)* Could we have some more lights, please? *(The stage lights come up full.)* And kill the storm. I think I'll save the rain till closer to the end of the scene, any-way. *(The lightning, thunder and rain effects stop. To TONY and AL-LEGRA.)* You can take a break. I'll bring you back in a few minutes and introduce you properly. *(They nod to him, then exit UC and off UL. WALTER turns to the audience.)* Hello. You caught us at an in-tense moment. I was working on a little scene ... well ... you'll see it later. I'm a writer, a playwright to be exact. No, that's not entirely ac-curate. I represent a playwright; I'm his alter-ego, so to speak. It would probably help if I had a name.... Let's see ... writer's alter-ego ... alter ... alter ... I know — how about Walter? Close enough? Fine. We'll call me Walter. Here's the deal: I thought you might find it in-teresting to see how I commit a murder. That's an offer you don't get every day, do you? The easiest way to show you is to deconstruct the crime, so that's what we're going to do. Now, pay attention; once you see how simple it is to knock somebody off, you might want to try it yourself ... in your imagination, of course. When I start a new play, the first thing I try to picture is the setting. I'm partial to old mansions like this one that's dark and gloomy. *(The lights dip down to the level they were before.)* A room such as this creates the perfect ambiance for a murder to occur, don't you think? I like fireplaces and French doors, and use them often. When the room lights go out, glowing em-bers and pale moonlight provide just the right amount of low lighting to evoke a sinister atmosphere. For example ... *(The lights go out as embers fade up at the fireplace and pale moonlight comes up at the French doors.)* See what I mean? It sort of makes you want to pull out a gun or knife or garrote, doesn't it? And as you just saw, the French doors also work great if you wish to throw in a thunderstorm. *(The moonlight changes to lightning flashes as rain and thunder sound ef-fects join in.)* Pretty chilling, huh? I've learned to keep the storm ef-fects to a minimum, though — if they go on too long, people start popping up in the audience and rushing out to the rest rooms. That can be terribly distracting. *(Calling out.)* Eighty-six the storm! *(The storm effects cease and the stage lights fade back up.)* That's better. *(Pointing to an audience member.)* I got the feeling you were just about to take off up the aisle. If you could hold it till intermission, I'd be extremely grateful. *(To all the audience as he moves UC to the archway.)* To get back to the subject, sliding doors are good, especially for sudden entrances, and I usually show the base of a staircase beyond so you get the sense that the house is at least two stories high. The characters can come and go up and down them to their bedrooms, presumably. A passageway here gives them entrances and exits to the kitchen and other rooms downstairs. Off up-right there is a door; its purpose is to create the sound effect for people coming into and going out of the house. *(We hear the door open and close.)* See? Another door above the fireplace leading to a parlor provides yet another access for the murderer to do his thing ... or hers, should I choose to use it for that purpose. When it comes to killers, I'm an equal opportunity playwright. *(Crossing back to DC.)* That brings us to the subject of suspects. I'd like you to meet the possible murderers in tonight's little mystery/comedy. There are quite a few of them. I mean, it wouldn't be much fun trying to guess who the killer is if there were only a couple of suspects to choose from, would it? Let's start with the characters you saw earlier. *(Calling out.)* Tony! Allegra! Hey, guys, come on back in. *(As he continues, TONY and ALLEGRA enter UC from off UL and cross to DR where they'll stand, facing out. ALLEGRA is a beautiful, scheming woman in her early 40's. TONY is a self-centered, handsome playboy in his early 30's.)* Oh, I need to tell you that this is the living room of powerful and ruthless millionaire, Edward Worthington the third. You'd be surprised how much time I put into thinking up just the right names for my plays' characters. "Edward Worthington" fits a mature man with a strong personality, doesn't it? ... and "the third" suggests old money handed down through several generations. Admit it, you wouldn't conjure up that image if I had named him "Jack Sprat," now would you? You'll meet Edward later. As you'll discover, most of the other characters have very strong feelings toward the man, including these two. This is Edward's wife, Allegra — his second wife, to be precise. *(To ALLEGRA.)* Help me out.

ALLEGRA. *(To the audience.)* When Edward grew tired of his first wife, Justine, he divorced her and married me. It's an old story: "Middle-aged Man Dumps First Spouse for Trophy Wife." *(To WALTER.)* I suppose I should be grateful you didn't name me "Heisman."

WALTER. Not a chance, my dear. Although I go for laughs, I do draw the line at low comedy. "Allegra" suits you perfectly. The name is beautiful and mysterious, like you.

ALLEGRA. Thank you. I shall do my best to live up to it.

TONY. *(To the audience.)* I'm Allegra's brother, Tony Blackwell. I'm a playboy. Can I help it if women find me irresistible? *(To a woman in the audience.)* How about meeting me after the show, gorgeous? I know this quiet little place where we can have an intimate supper for two. Afterward, we can go to my place, put on some romantic music, and then ....

WALTER. *(Cutting in.)* Time out! You had better not make any plans for later, Tony. If I decide to make you the murderer, you might find yourself in an intimate little jail cell.

TONY. That's true. *(To the woman.)* How about a rain check?

WALTER. *(To the audience.)* I use playboys in my shows fairly often. They invariably try to seduce one of the young women — a sweet, innocent maid, for example. That adds suspense to the story — will she succumb to his charms, or won't she? That's called a subplot. *(To the woman.)* At any rate, let me warn you, madam, if you do make a date with Tony, I absolve myself of all responsibility for his actions, once the play is over. I can control him here on the stage, but out there in the real world, well .... *(He shrugs.)* Moving right along.... Why don't you two be seated while I continue the introductions? *(TONY and ALLEGRA sit at the table SR. Calling out.)* Justine! Debra! *(JUSTINE and DEBRA enter SR through the French doors and cross to DC, joining him. Both wear coats over their dresses. JUSTINE is a bitter woman in her late 40's. DEBRA is a pretty college student in her 20's.)* Allegra mentioned Justine Worthington, Edward's ex-wife. This is she and their daughter, Debra, a college student. Justine, what are your feelings toward your former husband?

JUSTINE. I despise the ....

WALTER. *(Cutting in.)* Remember! This is a G-rated show!

JUSTINE. ...old goat! *(To the audience.)* When we married, I was young and attractive. I gave Edward a lovely daughter, Debra... *(Putting an arm around DEBRA.)*... but when I failed to provide him a male heir he could mold to become as heartless and power-hungry as he is, he made my life a living ... nightmare.

DEBRA. *(Hugging her.)* Poor Mom. *(To the audience.)* Father didn't mistreat me, he ignored me. When I was six or seven years old,

I had long curls that fell to my waist. One day I took a pair of scissors and chopped off all my hair, down to a one inch burr cut. That was years before girls ever considered such a style.

JUSTINE. *(Touching DEBRA's hair.)* Your beautiful curls ....

DEBRA. I thought if I looked like a boy, then maybe Father would pay attention to me. I don't think he even noticed ....

JUSTINE. I might have been able to forgive Edward for what he did to me, but his behavior toward our daughter ... I'll resent him for that till the day I die ... or he does!

WALTER. We get the picture. Be seated, ladies. *(JUSTINE and DEBRA cross SL where JUSTINE sits on the chair and DEBRA on the fireplace bench. WALTER crosses to DR, saying:)* Edward has one other family member, his sister, Beatrice Worthington. Beatrice is several years older than Edward and helped raise him since their parents were jet-setters who were constantly zipping around the globe, leaving their offspring at home in the care of nursemaids and servants. *(Calling out.)* Beatrice! Beatrice is somewhat befuddled, and it's possible her brother allows her to live in his household more from a sense of duty than any feelings of affection for his sibling.

(BEATRICE enters UC from off UL. She is a befuddled woman in her 60's.)

BEATRICE. Did somebody call me?

WALTER. Yes, Miss Worthington. Come down, please, and say hello to these nice people.

BEATRICE. *(Crossing to DC.)* People? *(To the audience.)* Oh, hello. It's so nice to see you. I don't go out much, so I rarely get to meet anyone except Edward's associates who call occasionally, and I never seem to understand what they're talking about. *(She frowns.)* Oh, dear.... *(To WALTER.)* I didn't realize so many guests were coming to Edward's birthday party. I don't think we have nearly enough food.

WALTER. Don't fret, Miss Worthington; they won't be joining us for dinner.

BEATRICE. Good. Oh, dear.... *(To the audience.)* It isn't that you're not welcome ....

WALTER. *(To the audience.)* Consider yourself lucky. Stage food is seldom what it's supposed to be — mashed bananas for whipped potatoes, that sort of thing. Starving actors usually love dinner scenes and will eat anything that's not nailed down, but still there are some food substitutions even they shudder to think about. *(To BEATRICE.)* You did very nicely, Miss Worthington. Why don't you join Allegra and Tony at the table?

BEATRICE. Alright ....

(She sits at the table SR.)

WALTER. As Beatrice mentioned, tonight's gathering is for a special occasion, Edward Worthington's birthday — his fiftieth, in fact. *(Crossing to DC.)* If you're wondering why his former wife would be present at this event, it's because Justine was ordered to, and since Edward signs her alimony checks, she bit the bullet and showed up. The birthday boy and his current wife have not been getting along lately; I suspect he wished to have Justine present to remind Allegra how easily he can "dispose" of her if she crosses him one time too many. I doubt if it's crossed his mind that Allegra could get fed up and "dispose" of him in a different way. Baby brother Tony would be only too willing to help her. But I digress.... Let me bring out the other party guests. *(Calling out.)* Roy! Connie! *(As WALTER crosses to DL, ROY and CONNIE enter at the French doors and cross to DC. ROY is an up-tight, nervous man in his 40's. CONNIE is a giddy woman in her 30's.)* Roy Phillips is Edward's business manager. He is responsible for overseeing Edward's vast fortune which includes the money he inherited as well as the millions generated yearly by Worthington Enterprises, a conglomerate of newspapers, television stations, and other media-related companies. It's a staggering responsibility that requires a serious-minded individual. No wonder Roy is always up-tight and displays all the warmth and humor of a Popsicle.

ROY. *(To WALTER.)* If Edward wants to laugh, he can hire a comedian. *(To the audience.)* I've worked for Edward for twenty years. My employer is brilliant at running his businesses, but he depends on me totally to control his finances. Sometimes I wonder if he appreciates how well I do my job.

WALTER. I have no doubt you're great at it. *(To the audience.)* They say behind every great man stands a great woman....*(CONNIE takes a step behind ROY. To her.)* No, Connie, that's just a figure of speech.

CONNIE. I thought ... never mind.

(She steps back up beside ROY.)

WALTER. The woman behind Roy — figuratively speaking — is his wife, Connie. She and her husband are as mismatched as striped pants with a plaid shirt. Connie is as giddy as Roy is somber.

CONNIE. *(To WALTER.)* Oh, I'm not that bad. *(To the audience.)* He's only saying that because I got lost in a super Wal-Mart for an entire day. It could happen to anybody.

WALTER. To be fair, I will add that she spent part of that time searching for her car in the parking lot.

CONNIE. *(To the audience.)* You've done that too, right?

WALTER. Roy, if you'll help Connie find her way over to the sofa, we'll continue. *(ROY takes CONNIE's arm; they cross to the sofa SL and sit.)* Another guest tonight is Edward's personal secretary, Peggy Sue Brumley. *(Calling out.)* Peggy Sue! *(PEGGY SUE enters UC from off UR. She is an attractive Southern belle in her 20's.)* Peggy Sue comes from Alabama, possibly with a banjo on her knee. I say that because Peggy Sue is your typical Southern belle. She goes by both her first and middle names, of course. South of the Mason-Dixon Line you'll find lots of Peggy Sue's, Peggy Jean's, Peggy Lee's, Peggy Ann's, whatever.

PEGGY SUE. *(To WALTER, with a strong Southern accent.)* That helps you tell all us Peggy's apart, sugar lump.

WALTER. *(Matching her accent.)* Well, shut my mouth! Say hi to all the folks, honey chile.

PEGGY SUE. *(To the audience.)* Hi, y'all.

WALTER. *(Dropping the accent.)* I confess I have a great affection for Southern women. They're charming, funny, and very bright, though they're good at hiding that fact when they want to. They could easily get away with murder because you'd never suspect a sweet young thing like Peggy Sue could be capable of a gristly crime.

PEGGY SUE. *(To WALTER.)* Well, I certainly hope not! *(To the audience.)* I don't know why Walter would even suggest such a thing. Murder, indeed! The very idea just gives me the willies! Besides, you'd have to dislike someone heaps and heaps to want them dead, and I get along fine with everybody ... *(Glancing at ALLEGRA.)* ... well, just about.

WALTER. And Edward?

PEGGY SUE. *(To WALTER.)* Edward? Edward can be extremely demanding at times, and real rude when he's in a bad mood ... and he gets in bad moods a lot. I admit he does ruffle my feathers sometimes ... *(To the audience.)* ... but you can't murder a person for having an unpleasant disposition, can you?

WALTER. Anything's possible. How about joining the family at the table, Peggy Sue?

PEGGY SUE. Sure, sweetie.

(She sits at the table SR.)

WALTER. I have one last business associate of Edward's to introduce. *(Calling out.)* Lawrence! *(LAWRENCE enters descending the stairs and comes to DC. LAWRENCE is a businesslike man in his 50's.)* Lawrence Tate is a lawyer, but that doesn't necessarily make him the villain of the piece. There is no doubt the man knows how to draw up a legal paper. *(Crossing to LAWRENCE DC.)* If Lawrence had been around in 1776, he could have whipped out the Declaration of Independence in fifteen minutes.

LAWRENCE. *(To WALTER.)* Thank you. I accept the compliment because it happens to be true. *(To the audience.)* You might say I'm especially adept at drafting the modern equivalent of the Declaration of Independence, to wit: divorce papers. If you don't believe me, just ask Justine Worthington. It's also possible that Allegra Worthington might be able to attest to that fact in the near future. Also, both women have learned the hard way that I can write a marriage contract that is iron-clad, one that protects Edward from fortune hunters with complete success.

WALTER. Thank you for the information, Lawrence.

LAWRENCE. Anytime. You'll receive my bill in the mail.

(He crosses to the chair UR and sits.)

WALTER. *(To the audience.)* I have only myself to blame — I created him. *(Crossing to DR.)* One more set of introductions, then we'll get this show on the road: the servants. *(Calling out.)* Staff! Please join us! *(INA enters at the archway from off UL; HOLLISTER enters at the archway from off UR; MRS. VICKERS enters UL; EDITH ENTERS descending the stairs. HOLLISTER is a formal man in his 60's; MRS. VICKERS is an outspoken woman in her 40's; INA, who has a quick temper, is in her 40's; EDITH is a pretty, shy girl in her 20's. They all cross to DC. WALTER continues to the audience.)* In real life, it would take a staff the size of a small platoon to run a mansion as large as Worthington Manor, but for our purposes, these four will represent the servants quite nicely. Sound off, troops.

(All four address the audience.)

HOLLISTER. I am Hollister, the butler. I picture Worthington Manor as a huge ocean liner of which I am the captain. The other servants can tell you I run a tight ship.

MRS. VICKERS. That's the truth, and I like it that way. I am Mrs. Vickers, the housekeeper. Mr. Worthington's home is a showplace, and I intend to keep it that way.

INA. I'm Ina, the cook. *(Cutting her eyes at WALTER.)* Somebody didn't give me a last name, so it's just Ina. I do my job, keep my ears open, and mouth shut. You'd be surprised what I could tell you about the people who live under this roof … but I won't.

EDITH. I'm Edith, the maid. I'm kind of shy, and I wish I didn't have to stand up here and talk about myself. *(To WALTER.)* I heard what you said about Mr. Tony trying to seduce maids, and that makes me nervous, too.

WALTER. Don't worry, my dear. We'll deal with Tony when the time comes. *(Crossing to DC.)* If I may take center stage? *(The SERVANTS cross above the sofa and stand. To the audience.)* Here you have them — the cast of characters in tonight's little mystery … well, most of them. They include, as you recall, Edward's current wife and her playboy brother, his ex-wife and their daughter, his sister, his business manager and his wife, his secretary, his lawyer, and the household staff. They'll start the play while I summon Edward Worthington, the key figure in our story. *(Calling out.)* Could we have a blackout and some mood music to provide the transition, please?

(The lights fade out. Somber music comes in and plays in the darkness as the cast clears offstage.)

ACT I

Scene 1

(After a few beats, the music fades out as the light in the foyer fades up. It is night. Moonlight fades up behind the French doors; it will fade out as clouds pass over the moon. Embers glow in the fireplace. MRS. VICKERS enters UC from off UL. She stops and snaps the light switch at the side of the archway. The room lights come up. She surveys the room, then crosses to the sofa and plumps up a pillow on it. EDITH enters UC from off UL, carrying a tray of hors d'oeuvres.)

EDITH. Ina sent me in with the hors d'oeuvres, Mrs. Vickers.

MRS. VICKERS. Put them on the table, Edith, though I doubt anyone will have much of an appetite.

EDITH. *(Crossing to the table SR and putting down the tray.)* That would be a shame. Ina has prepared a wonderful dinner: pot roast, gravy, whipped potatoes ....

(MRS. VICKERS gives an almost imperceptible shudder.)

MRS. VICKERS. She could have saved herself the trouble and opened a can of Spam. Believe me, this crowd won't have their mind on the cooking.

EDITH. What do you mean?

MRS. VICKERS. I mean the guests know Mr. Worthington wouldn't call them here for the pleasure of their company. He's barely civil to them, at best. You mark my words, the boss is up to something.

EDITH. I hope it doesn't get unpleasant. I hate scenes.

MRS. VICKERS. Then you'd better find a broom closet to take shelter in. I know Mr. Worthington, and I know what he's capable of.

(INA leads BEATRICE in UC from off UL. BEATRICE has a cloth napkin tucked into her neckline like a bib.)

INA. You come on in here, Miss Beatrice. Hollister will announce dinner when it's ready. *(To MRS. VICKERS and EDITH.)* I found her sitting at the dinning room table with a knife in one hand and a fork in the other. *(Removing the napkin.)* I'll take this.

BEATRICE. I'm hungry.

MRS. VICKERS. *(Joining them UC.)* There's a tray of Ina's lovely hors d'oeuvres on the table, Miss Beatrice. Why don't you have some of those?

BEATRICE. I believe I will.

(She sits US at the table SR. She will slowly and methodically nibble hors d'oeuvres, ignoring the servants.)

INA. I have to get back to my Brussels sprouts. Edith, come with me. *(With a look at BEATRICE.)* You'd better bring in another tray of hors d'oeuvres.

EDITH. Yes, m'am.

INA. *(To MRS. VICKERS.)* If you can keep her in here, I'd appreciate it.

MRS. VICKERS. I think she'll be content where she is.

(INA nods to MRS. VICKERS.)

INA. Edith …

(She and EDITH exit UC and off UL.)

MRS. VICKERS. Miss Beatrice, I need you to sit right here and wait for the others. They'll be here shortly. I have to check the parlor should anyone wish to retire there after dinner.

BEATRICE. Hum? Retire? *(Starting to rise.)* Is it time to go to bed?

MRS. VICKERS. *(Pushing her gently back down.)* No, Miss Beatrice. Just ... enjoy your snack.

BEATRICE. Snack? Oh, yes.... Do you want some? You can have the ones with the black things.

MRS. VICKERS. They're olives.

BEATRICE. I don't like them. You eat them.

MRS. VICKERS. No, thank you. There are some lovely mints, too. I'll check on you later. *(She crosses to UL, muttering to herself.)* That poor woman ....

(She exits UL. BEATRICE picks up the mint dish, looks around, rises, crosses to the table UL, pours the mints into a vase there, blows on the dish, puts it into her pocket, then returns to the table and sits. She picks up an hors d'oeuvre and removes a slice of black olive from it.)

BEATRICE. *(Muttering.)* Nasty ....

(She drops it onto the floor beside her chair, then eats the hors d'oeuvre. ALLEGRA and TONY enter UC, descending the stairs. Each is carrying a gift-wrapped package.)

TONY. I feel like a hypocrite. Besides, what do you give someone who makes more money in a day than you do in a lifetime? A doormat everyone can kneel on to kiss his feet?

ALLEGRA. I think he owns several already. What did you get him?

TONY. A necktie; it's the closest thing to a noose I could think of. What about you?

ALLEGRA. A gold-plated pen and pencil set. Since everything Edward touches turns to gold anyway, I thought they would be appropriate.

(They come into the room. ALLEGRA will simply tolerate BEATRICE.)

BEATRICE. Presents:.... Are those for me?

ALLEGRA. No, Beatrice, they're for your brother. It's Edward's birthday.

BEATRICE. It is? That's right, it is. Oh, dear, I forgot to buy bubba a present, but I could give him a little something I happened to pick up.

ALLEGRA. That's not necessary. *(Taking TONY's gift.)* I'll put these over here.

(She crosses to the table UL and puts them there.)

TONY. Hors d'oeuvres.... They look good.
BEATRICE. Most of them are.

(She rises, takes the tray, and carries it possessively to the sofa where she sits on the SL end, putting the tray on the coffee table.)

TONY. I'm not very hungry anyway.

(He notices the olive slice on the floor and stomps on it.)

ALLEGRA. *(Crossing to him.)* What is it?
TONY. Some kind of beetle, I think. It must have come in at the French doors.

(Unnoticed by them, BEATRICE removes another slice of olive from an hors d'oeuvre, drops it on the floor by the sofa, and eats the hors d'oeuvre. She will continue to nibble. Meanwhile, ALLEGRA crosses to the French doors and makes sure they're closed properly. TONY wipes his shoe on the rug.)

ALLEGRA. It's clouding over. The TV weatherman said there's a storm approaching.
TONY. How appropriate. It could get tempestuous inside as well as out.
ALLEGRA. Tony! Edward has been very difficult to deal with lately. Try not to do anything that might upset him.
TONY. I'll try, sister dear, but the very fact that I breathe the

same air seems to upset Edward.

(EDITH enters UC from off UL, carrying another tray of hor d'oeuvres.)

EDITH. Excuse me. *(She takes a step SL, then stops when she sees the other tray is now on the coffee table. Confused.) Oh ....*
BEATRICE. *(Noticing EDITH.)* More nibbles.... How nice!
EDITH. I'll ... uh ... I'll put these over here.

(She crosses to the table SR and puts down the tray.)

TONY. *(Moving next to EDITH.)* You're looking very pretty to-night, Edith.
ALLEGRA. *(Sarcastic.)* It must be the dress.
EDITH. *(Nervous.)* Thank you, Mr. Blackwell. You look nice in your tuxedo, and all ....
ALLEGRA. Edith, I imagine Ina could come up with something for you to do in the kitchen. Why don't you find out?
EDITH. Yes, m'am.

(She hurries out UC and off UL.)

ALLEGRA. *(Crossing to TONY.)* Really, Tony, leave the girl alone. You'd be better off trying to charm some young heiress who could support you. I don't think Edward is going to allow me to help you out much longer.
TONY. The old skinflint! But don't worry, Allegra, I have enough charm to go around for both heiresses and pretty maids. *(The doorbell.)* Ah, the guests are starting to arrive.

(The doorbell rings again.)

BEATRICE. Is the Avon lady here?
ALLEGRA. No, Beatrice. Eat your hors d'oeuvres.
BEATRICE. What a good idea.

(She goes back to munching. She will discard another olive slice

along the way. ALLEGRA straightens TONY's tie as HOLLISTER enters UC from off UL, crosses past the archway, and exits off UR. We hear the door open.)

HOLLISTER. *(Off UR.)* Come in. *(The door closes.)* Let me hang your coats.
ROY. *(Off UR.)* Thank you, Hollister.
TONY. *(Under his breath to ALLEGRA.)* The life of the party is here.

(HOLLISTER enters UC from off UR with ROY and CONNIE, who is holding a present.)

HOLLISTER. The Phillips.

(He takes the present from CONNIE, sees the others on the table UL, crosses there and puts the present on it, then will exit through the archway and off UL. Meanwhile, ROY and CONNIE come into the room. TONY and ALLEGRA cross to them. TONY extends his hand toward ROY.)

TONY. Hey, Roy, old boy!

(ROY looks disdainfully at TONY's hand a beat, then gives it a quick shake.)

ROY. Tony. Allegra.
ALLEGRA. Roy ... Connie.
CONNIE. *(Grabbing ALLEGRA's hands in hers.)* Allegra, you look beautiful! I love that dress! I wish I could find one like it!
ALLEGRA. I don't think they carry Armani at Wal-Mart.
CONNIE. You might be right, but I'll ask the next time I'm there.
ALLEGRA. You do that.
ROY. Where is our host?
ALLEGRA. He'll be down shortly. Make yourselves comfortable. I'll get us something to drink.

(She crosses to the archway and pulls the bell cord.)

TONY. Care for an hors d'oeuvre?

CONNIE. I don't mind if I do. *(Crossing to the sofa.)* Good evening, Miss Beatrice. May I join you?

BEATRICE. I guess so.... *(CONNIE sits on the sofa beside her. ROY and TONY nibble hors d'oeuvres from the tray on the table SR. BEATRICE revolves the tray, turning the hors d'oeuvres with olive slices toward CONNIE.)* Eat the ones with the black things.

(CONNIE eats an hors d'oeuvre. EDITH enters UC from off UL.)

EDITH. You rang, Mrs. Worthington?

ALLEGRA. Yes, Edith. You can begin to serve the wine.

EDITH. Yes, m'am.

(She exits off UL.)

TONY. So, Roy, how are things at the office?

ROY. Under control.

(The doorbell rings.)

TONY. I don't doubt it in the least.

(HOLLISTER enters UC from off UL, crosses past the archway, and exits off UR.)

ROY. How are things ... wherever it is you spend your time?

TONY. Couldn't be better, Roy, couldn't be better.

(The door opens off UR.)

HOLLISTER. *(Off UR.)* Come in, Miss Brumley. *(The door closes.)* I'll take your coat.

ALLEGRA. *(Muttering to herself.)* I'll have to get Edith to bring in some Southern Comfort.

PEGGY SUE. *(Off UR.)* Thanks a bunch, Hollister. Here, be a lamb and hold this.

ALLEGRA. Or maybe a pint of Jack Daniels.

(HOLLISTER enters UC with PEGGY SUE from off UR. He is holding a gift that is so large that when he pauses in the archway facing DS, he is hidden behind it from the waist up.)

HOLLISTER. Miss Brumley.

(He will cross to the table SL, put the gift there, then exit through the archway and off UL. By this point, the moonlight has faded out.)

PEGGY SUE. 'Evening, everybody!

CONNIE. My goodness, Peggy Sue, that's the biggest present I have ever seen! What is it?

TONY. For Edward? Probably a money clip.

PEGGY SUE. *(Giggling.)* Silly! Actually, it's a year's supply of caramel corn? *(Sometimes PEGGY SUE's statements will end with a question mark; that rising inflection at the end is a good ol' Southern trait.)* The clerk assured me it wouldn't get stale.

ALLEGRA. What does he care? He probably retired after he made that sale.

PEGGY SUE. Oh, it didn't cost a whole heap, Allegra, honey. It's a token gift, anyway. Edward already has everything his little ol' heart desires.

ALLEGRA. *(Giving her a steady look.)* Does he, now? *(PEGGY SUE returns the look a beat, then turns to the men and smiles.)* Roy, Tony, y'all look mighty spiffy tonight.

TONY. So do you, Peggy Sue.

ROY. Good evening.

TONY. In fact, they ought to outlaw a dress like that on a woman like you. I'd say the combination could be highly combustible.

PEGGY SUE. *(Giggles.)* Flatterer.

(EDITH enters UC from off UL, carrying a tray of wine glasses.)

EDITH. Wine?
ALLEGRA. Not a moment too soon.

(She snatches a glass from the tray and drinks.)

PEGGY SUE. *(Taking a glass.)* I wouldn't mind a little bubbly.

*(ROY and TONY take glasses. TONY gives EDITH a wink. She turns,
flustered, and crosses to the sofa.)*

EDITH. Mrs. Phillips?
CONNIE. *(Taking a glass.)* Thank you, Edith. Miss Beatrice,
would you care for a glass?
BEATRICE. What's in it?
CONNIE. Wine.
BEATRICE. Nope. If it's not Sprite, I don't want it.
ALLEGRA. Run along, Edith, and set up round two.
EDITH. Yes, m'am.

(She hurries out UC and off UL.)

CONNIE. Roy, come join us.
ROY. Yes, dear.

(He crosses and sits on the sofa by CONNIE.)

TONY. Peggy Sue?

(He pulls out the chair SR of the table.)

PEGGY SUE. Why, thank you, Tony.

(She sits. He sits US of the table. The doorbell rings.)

ALLEGRA. That must be Lawrence. Everyone else is here.

*(HOLLISTER enters UC from off UL, crosses the archway, then exits

off UR. The door opens.)

HOLLISTER. *(Off UR.)* Mr. Tate, please come in.
TONY. You were right, Allegra.
ALLEGRA. It had to be he or the delivery boy from Domino's ... *(The door closes .)* ... and I know for a fact Ina cooked a roast, gravy, whipped potatoes ....

(Everyone gives an almost imperceptible shudder.)

HOLLISTER. *(Off UR.)* This way ... *(He enters UC from off UR, followed by LAWRENCE who carries a briefcase.)* ... Mr. Tate.

(HOLLISTER exits off UL.)

ALLEGRA. Good evening, Lawrence.
LAWRENCE. Allegra ... everyone....
ROY. Good grief, Lawrence, why do you have your briefcase? This is a party. Have you got to the point where you've attached that thing to your wrist with handcuffs like a diplomatic courier?
LAWRENCE. No, Roy. There are some papers inside that Edward insisted I bring him. *(He opens the briefcase and takes out a small gift which he hands to ALLEGRA.)* This is for him as well. If you'll excuse me, he asked me to join him in his suite as soon as I arrived.

(He ascends the stairs and exits.)

ALLEGRA. *(Putting the gift on the table UL.)* How typical of Edward — he never stops thinking of business, even on his birthday.

(There is a low, distant rumble of thunder.)

CONNIE. What was that?
BEATRICE. If someone's stomach is growling, they can eat the snacks with the black things on them.

TONY. It was thunder. At least everyone arrived before the storm.

ALLEGRA. Yes, everyone is here.

(The French doors open and JUSTINE and DEBRA enter. They wear coats over their dresses. DEBRA is carrying a present.)

JUSTINE. Now everyone is here.

ALLEGRA. Justine! Who invited you to the party?

JUSTINE. Edward, and he didn't invite me, he ordered me to be here.

DEBRA. Father told me to drive down from college as well. Since he pays the tuition, I didn't have much choice, did I?

(They cross to ALLEGRA UC.)

BEATRICE. *(Waving at DEBRA.)* Hello, Debra, dear.

DEBRA. Hello, Aunt Bea.

(She crosses to above the sofa, kisses BEATRICE's cheek, then puts the gift on the table UL. As this happens:)

CONNIE. Justine, dear, why didn't you come to the front door? Did you get lost?

JUSTINE. No, Connie, *my* sense of direction is fine. I didn't care to have Hollister greet me at the door like a guest. This used to be my home, and he used to be my butler. The situation would be awkward for both of us. I preferred to let myself in.

DEBRA. Come on, Mom, let's hang up our coats.

(They exit UC and off UR. MRS. VICKERS enters UL.)

MRS. VICKERS. I've set out games in the parlor if anyone cares to play after dinner.

ALLEGRA. Mrs. Vickers, Justine and Debra Worthington just arrived unexpectedly. I'm afraid we'll need two more places set at the dining table.

MRS. VICKERS. It's done; I knew they were coming.
ALLEGRA. Why didn't you tell me?
MRS. VICKERS. You didn't ask.

(EDITH enters UC from off UL with a tray of wine glasses.)

EDITH. More wine, anyone? *(ALLEGRA abruptly sets her empty glass on the tray and picks up a fresh one. JUSTINE and DEBRA enter UC from off UR, without coats.)* Why, Mrs. Worthington ... I mean the other one ... and Miss Debra ... would you care for some wine?
JUSTINE. *(Taking a glass.)* Thanks.
DEBRA. *(Taking a glass.)* Thank you, Edith.
MRS. VICKERS. Put the tray on the table, Edith, then help me check the dining room one last time.
EDITH. Yes, Mrs. Vickers.

(She puts the tray on the table SR.)

MRS. VICKERS. *(To ALLEGRA.)* You can ring if you need anything. Edith.

(MRS. VICKERS exits UC and off UL followed by EDITH.)

JUSTINE. Ina is a great cook, so at least we'll get a decent meal out of this fiasco. What's for dinner?
TONY. Roast beef, gravy, whipped potatoes ....

(Everyone gives an almost imperceptible shudder.)

JUSTINE. *(Not terribly convincing.)* That sounds good ....
PEGGY SUE. Debra, darlin', why don't you and your mother join us? Sit a spell.
DEBRA. Alright.

(She sits SL at the table SR.)

JUSTINE. This will do fine.

(She sits on the chair DR of the sofa.)

ALLEGRA. *(Crossing SL to the fireplace.)* My, my, what a gathering. Edward's loving family and dearest friends. *(She laughs.)* What a joke!

BEATRICE. Did someone tell a joke? I must have missed it.

ALLEGRA. Don't worry about it, Beatrice. *(She suddenly stomps the olive slices on the floor. Muttering.)* I have to tell Mrs. Vickers to call the Orkin man.

(LAWRENCE enters descending the stairs, with the briefcase. He will stop at the archway.)

LAWRENCE. Edward is coming down.

PEGGY SUE. *(Rising.)* Get up, everybody! We have to toast the birthday boy! *(Taking another glass from the tray.)* Here, Lawrence. *(He crosses to her and takes the glass. Everyone who is seated rises and faces the archway. BEATRICE looks confused, then picks up an hors d'oeuvre to toast with. EDWARD enters, descending the stairs. When his head becomes visible, we see that the role is being played by WALTER who has donned a tuxedo, added silver to his temples, and put on a pair of glasses. When he stops at the archway, all raise their glasses — and hors d'oeuvre — except JUSTINE and DEBRA who simply hold their glasses but don't toast.)* Happy birthday, Edward!

CONNIE. Cheers!

EDWARD. Hold it! *(The others freeze. To the audience, speaking as WALTER.)* A playwright performs all the roles in his head as he writes the show. I needed a really good actor to play this part, so I thought I'd jump in and do Edward for you. *(To the others.)* Carry on.

(They break the freeze.)

CONNIE. Hip! Hip!
THE OTHERS. Hooray!

(JUSTINE and DEBRA say the word without enthusiasm.)

BEATRICE. Hip! Hip! Hip...?
ALLEGRA. Forget it, Beatrice. Two "hips" are enough for anybody.
EDWARD. I see you all managed to arrive. Good. I promise you
this will be a night you'll all remember.

*(There is a rumble of thunder, louder than before. PEGGY SUE takes
    a glass from the tray and crosses to EDWARD.)*

PEGGY SUE. *(Handing him the glass.)* Here, Edward, sugar, you
need a glass of wine.
EDWARD. Thank you, Peggy Sue.
PEGGY SUE. Happy birthday, darlin'.

(She kisses his cheek. ALLEGRA bristles.)

EDWARD. Sit down, everyone. I have an announcement to
make. *(He pulls the bell cord. The others sit where they were, except
PEGGY SUE sits DS of the table SR; LAWRENCE takes her chair SR
of the table; ALLEGRA sits on the SL sofa arm.)* When a man reaches
the half-century mark, it makes him think. Where have I been? Where
am I going? What do I plan to do with the rest of my life?

(EDITH enters UC from off UL.)

EDITH. You rang, Mr. Worthington?
EDWARD. Yes, Edith. Tell the other servants I wish to see all of
you, in here, now.
EDITH. Yes, sir.

(She exits off UL. EDWARD will cross around the sofa and to DL.)

EDWARD. As I was saying, what do I plan to do with the rest of
my life? I intend to make some important changes, for one thing.
TONY. Changes? What kind of changes?
EDWARD. That's precisely what I've brought you all together to
discuss.

(HOLLISTER, MRS. VICKERS, INA and EDITH enter UC from off UL. They'll spread across the archway.)

HOLLISTER. Edith informed us you wished to see us, Mr. Worthington.

EDWARD. Yes, Hollister. I wanted all of my family, closest business associates and servants present while I make an announcement. *(Crossing slowly to DR.)* Everyone in this room depends on me to provide them a living, and thus far I've provided for all of you very well. You would think my generosity would gain me your appreciation, if not affection. Apparently, though, what someone here feels is resentment, perhaps even hatred. *(Turning back to face them.)* It has come to my attention that one amongst you is a traitor.

(The others react, looking at one another and ad-libbing denials.)

ROY. You suspect one of us is your enemy?

EDWARD. I don't suspect, I know ... and I have proof. Lawrence.... *(LAWRENCE opens the briefcase and takes out a thick, business-size envelope, closed with a wax seal. EDWARD crosses to him.)* I had Lawrence bring me this. Inside is the evidence of the traitor's duplicity. I promise you, before the evening is over, this person will pay dearly!

ALLEGRA. Edward, if you're planning to ... punish ... one of us in some way, why not do whatever you're going to do now and get it over with?

MRS. VICKERS. I was wondering the same thing, Mr. Worthington, if you don't mind my saying so.

EDWARD. I intend to let this ... worm ... squirm a while before squashing it. I see you've brought me some gifts. After dinner I'll open them, concluding with this ... *(The envelope.)* ... my birthday present to myself. That is when I'll rid myself of a back-stabbing sycophant once and for all. *(There is a rumble of thunder close by. EDWARD puts the envelope into an inside pocket of the tux coat.)* But for now, let the festivities begin. What are we having for dinner, Ina?

INA. Your favorites, sir. Roast beef, gravy, whipped potatoes ....

(Everyone gives an almost imperceptible shudder.)

EDWARD. I can hardly wait. It sounds like a dinner to die for.

(There is a flash of lightning and crash of thunder. The lights lower quickly to a BLACKOUT. Somber music fades in for the scene change. The trays of hors d'oeuvres, wine glass tray, wine glasses and briefcase are struck. The cast, except EDWARD, exits. He crosses to the French doors.)

Scene 2

(The music fades out as the lights fade up. EDWARD is looking out the French doors. There is a flash of distant lightning, followed by thunder. The embers have burned out.)

EDWARD. *(Turning to the audience and removing his glasses, speaking as WALTER.)* As you've no doubt guessed, that was a blackout to show the end of Act One, Scene One. In my mysteries, that's the scene where I usually introduce you to the characters in the play and give you an idea of their relationships to one another. This is called "exposition." In tonight's production, the scene was shorter than usual since they and I told you something about them before the play began. Now let's get into Scene Two, about two hours later. This is the scene where the plot thickens ... make that, "the plot, like gravy, thickens." I had to get the full title in there. Act One, Scene Two ....

(He puts the glasses back on and turns back to the French doors. Thunder and lightning. PEGGY SUE enters UL and crosses to UC.)

PEGGY SUE. Edward, darlin', what'cha doing in here all by

your lonesome? Nearly everybody's in the parlor playing games till you're ready to open the gifts and make your announcement. Well, they're going through the motions — nobody's really interested in Monopoly or Clue.

EDWARD. I know a better game. *(Crossing to her.)* Why don't you and I slip off and play one of our own ... in private?

(He touches her arm.)

PEGGY SUE. Uh-uh. *(Crossing past him to UR.)* We can't do that, sugar, not here. You know that.

EDWARD. I don't like being told "no," Peggy Sue. You know that!

PEGGY SUE. Now, now, don't lose your temper, sweetpea. Besides, for all I know, I might be the one you're planning to fire, or whatever.

EDWARD. You? Have you been up to no good, Peggy Sue?

PEGGY. Of course not! I would never do anything to hurt you, honey lamb, but someone could have told you I have been. Allegra, for instance? She hates me, you know. I just hate it when somebody hates me.

EDWARD. *(Crossing to her.)* Allegra has never said a word against you.

PEGGY SUE. If she hasn't, it's because she's afraid to. I'm sure she suspects I'm more to you than an employee, but she doesn't dare confront you about it. Allegra knows if she forced you to choose between us, you'd toss her aside like a used Kleenex.

EDWARD. You think so?

PEGGY SUE. Well, sure! You told me you made her sign a pre-nuptial agreement before you'd marry her, didn't you, like the one Justine had to?

EDWARD. Of course. I'm too smart to let some fortune hunter take me for millions.

PEGGY SUE. But before you divorce them, your wives get to live like queens. Allegra has ridden the merry-go-round long enough. It's someone else's turn. Why who knows, you might have finally found a woman you'll want to live with the rest of your life?

EDWARD. We'll see, Peggy Sue. After tonight, there could be quite a few changes around here.

PEGGY SUE. Fine. If you'll excuse me, I need to slip into one of the upstairs bathrooms and freshen up. *(PEGGY SUE crosses to the archway.)* Don't you go and reveal your big surprise till I get back. *(Turning back.)* I don't suppose you'd give me hint who it is you plan to reprimand, would you?

EDWARD. I can't do that, Peggy Sue.

PEGGY SUE. Even if I pout?

EDWARD. Even if you pout.

PEGGY SUE. Well, then, I won't waste the pucker. They make little lines around your mouth, anyway. I'll be back in two shakes of a lamb's tail.

(She ascends the stairs and exits. Thunder and lightning. BEATRICE enters UL.)

BEATRICE. Here you are, Edward.

EDWARD. *(Crossing to UC.)* Were you looking for me, Beatrice?

BEATRICE. Yes ... I ....

EDWARD. What is it?

BEATRICE. *(Crossing to the sofa and sitting on the SL end.)* I listened to what you said to all of us earlier, but I'm confused.

EDWARD. I expected that.

BEATRICE. I think you're unhappy with one of us ...

EDWARD. *(Crossing to above the SR end of the sofa.)* At least one.

BEATRICE. ... and you're going to punish someone.

EDWARD. That's my plan.

BEATRICE. I hope it isn't me.

EDWARD. Have you been naughty?

BEATRICE. I don't think so. I try to be good. I try really hard.

EDWARD. Then what are you worried about?

BEATRICE. Those papers in the envelope you put in your pocket.... I'm afraid they're papers to ... what do you call them? ... to put me in a home.

EDWARD. Commitment papers.

BEATRICE. Yes, that's it. *(She grabs his hand.)* You wouldn't send me away, would you, little bubba? This is my home. I've lived here all my life, both of us have. I don't want to go anywhere else.

EDWARD. *(Withdrawing his hand and crossing to the archway.)* I'd hate to banish you, Beatrice, but if you've done something really bad and need to be punished ....

BEATRICE. I wouldn't! I haven't!

EDWARD. We'll see. *(He pulls the bell cord.)* Do you know a Mr. Jamison, Beatrice?

BEATRICE. Jamison? No, I don't think so ....

EDWARD. Paul Jamison.

BEATRICE. *(Frowning in concentration.)* Jamison ... Paul Jamison.... Oh, I know where I've heard that name. The other day when I walked into the library, your lawyer ... Mr. Tate? ... was on the phone. When he saw me, he said, "I'll get back to you, Jamison."

EDWARD. That's very interesting.

(HOLLISTER enters UC from off UL.)

HOLLISTER. Yes, Mr. Worthington?

EDWARD. My sister is tired, Hollister. I thought you might have Ina brew her a cup of tea to refresh her.

HOLLISTER. I'll be glad to. Miss Beatrice, why don't you come with me?

BEATRICE. With you? Of course. *(She rises and crosses to HOLLISTER who takes her arm gently.)* Where are we going, Hollister?

HOLLISTER. To the kitchen. We're going to have some tea.

BEATRICE. A tea party?

HOLLISTER. If you like.

BEATRICE. Oh, I would! I would!

HOLLISTER. You're wearing a very nice perfume, Miss Beatrice. Is it new?

BEATRICE. Yes, it's called primrose.

(They exit off UL.)

ROY. *(Off UL.)* It won't take but a few minutes.

LAWRENCE. *(Off UL.)* Oh, alright, if you insist. *(EDWARD exits through the archway, then pulls the sliding doors almost shut, leaving a small gap through which he eavesdrops. ROY and LAWRENCE enter UL. Thunder and lightning. LAWRENCE will cross to the fireplace to warm his hands. ROY will pace nervously CS.)* Drat! The embers have gone out. *(Turning to ROY.)* What's so important you pulled me away from the table? I own Boardwalk and Park Place. If someone lands on my property while I'm in here, I'll lose a fortune in rent.

ROY. For Pete's sake, Lawrence, that's just a game!

LAWRENCE. One that you were losing. I hope you do a better job of managing Edward's financial affairs than you do at Monopoly. So, what did you want to see me about?

ROY. Those papers Edward had you bring him tonight. What are they?

LAWRENCE. Good grief, Roy, you know I can't answer such a question. How long do you think Edward would retain me as his lawyer if I went around revealing privileged information?

ROY. It's just .... Look, you heard what he said about there being a "traitor" among the group here tonight. The thing is, I've transferred some of Edward's funds ... quite a sizable amount ... into a bank account in my name.

LAWRENCE. Why would you do that?

ROY. Because a major television station Edward has wanted to acquire for a long time is going on the market. If the owners knew he was interested, they'd double their asking price. I plan to make them an offer in my name. If they accept, I'll purchase it, then revert the property to Worthington Enterprises.

LAWRENCE. I see.

ROY. Yes, now that I've explained it. But if Edward noticed the money transfer and doesn't know why I did it ....

LAWRENCE. Say no more. Want some free advice? If I were you, I'd hang on to that "get out of jail free" card you drew.

ROY. This is no joking matter!

LAWRENCE. You're right. Why are you telling me this? Why not tell Edward?

ROY. If I'm not the one he suspects of betraying him, then

there's no need to bother him with it. He's never shown any interest in the details of how I invest his money before now.

LAWRENCE. And why call his attention to it if you don't have to, right?

ROY. Well ... yes .... So if you'll just tell me if those papers relate to me ....

LAWRENCE. I don't know.

ROY. What!?!

LAWRENCE. I have no idea what's in that envelope. Edward instructed me to go by his office on my way here, look in his desk drawer, and take out the blank envelope with the wax seal. He told me to bring it here and show him I have it, immediately upon arrival. That's what I did.

ROY. I assumed you knew ....

LAWRENCE. *(Cutting in.)* As did everyone else, I expect. Edward could have brought the envelope home himself. I figure that he had me bring it so that he could make a point of having me hand it to him, stir everybody up. The fact is, I'm as much in the dark as you are about its contents.

ROY. So they could relate to you as well as anyone.

LAWRENCE. Me? I haven't done anything to feel guilty about. My conscience is clear.

ROY. Is it? Is it, really?

(They stare at each other a beat. Thunder and lightning.)

CONNIE. *(Off UL.)* Roy? *(She enters UL, stopping above the sofa.)* The game's over. Justine won. I would have, but I hid my money and forgot where I put it. *(She gives a giddy laugh, putting her hand to her bosom.)* Oh, here it is! *(She reaches down the neck of her dress and brings out some Monopoly play money.)* Silly me! I must have deposited it in my bra. Now I'm flat busted! *(She laughs again. When the men don't join her, the laugh trails off.)* My goodness, you're a pair of gloomy Gusses. What's the matter?

ROY. Nothing. I'm going for a breath of fresh air.

(He crosses to the French doors and exits, leaving one ajar.)

CONNIE. But Roy, it's going to storm .... Oh, dear .... *(To LAW-RENCE.)* I wish he wouldn't go outside while it's lightning. He could be struck dead as a doornail ... whatever that is.

LAWRENCE. I guess he figures the wrath of Mother Nature is nothing compared to Edward's.

CONNIE. Huh?

(JUSTINE and DEBRA enter UL.)

JUSTINE. Lawrence ... we rolled for you and Roy. I took all your money. You went bankrupt.

LAWRENCE. So I heard.

(He sits on the bench.)

JUSTINE. *(Snatching the money from CONNIE.)* I think this belongs to me too. *(Crossing around the sofa and sitting.)* The way I see it, get it while you can. Edward taught me that.

DEBRA. *(Sitting beside her.)* Don't, Mom ....

JUSTINE. Don't worry, dear, I'll hold my temper ... at least until your father makes his announcement. After that, anything goes.

CONNIE. *(Crossing to the table SR and sitting on the SL chair.)* I wish he'd get it over with. I hate suspense. I love murder mysteries, but I always read the last chapter first to find out who did it.

JUSTINE. If you feel a rumble, it's Agatha Christie, spinning in her grave. *(Lightning and a huge crash of thunder.)* Calm down, Aggie.

CONNIE. Murders make me nervous, and when I get nervous, I break out in hives. It's just awful!

JUSTINE. I'm sure it is; it's a good thing calamine lotion is so cheap. So, Lawrence, how about telling us what's in the envelope Edward is carrying near where he heart would be, if he had one? I'll make it worth your while.

(She spreads the play money on the coffee table.)

LAWRENCE. Roy was wondering the same thing, just moments

ago. As I told him, I don't know.

DEBRA. You don't? I thought it might be ... never mind.

LAWRENCE. Why should you be concerned, Debra?

DEBRA. Father arranged for the college to send him a copy of my grades each semester — not that he cares about me, he's more interested in how his money is being spent. I've had some problems lately, and ... well ... I haven't done so hot in most of my classes.

(EDWARD slides the doors shut quietly, closing the gap.)

LAWRENCE. And you're worried that Edward might cut off your tuition?

DEBRA. Yes.

JUSTINE. If he tries it, I'll cut off his head!

CONNIE. Oh, my goodness!

(The door off UR opens and closes softly. The ones onstage don't hear it.)

LAWRENCE. We won't know what he's planning until he decides to tell us. Until then, the contents of that envelope will remain a mystery.

(CONNIE scratches her arm. Thunder and lightning. The sliding doors open, making everyone jump. PEGGY SUE is there.)

PEGGY SUE. I'm back, Eddie honey, fresh as a daisy! Oh ... I thought Edward was in here. Have y'all seen him?

JUSTINE. Not lately, which is how I like it.

LAWRENCE. After his announcement, he's been lying low.

JUSTINE. Not low enough — I'd prefer six feet under.

DEBRA. Mom, you don't mean that!

JUSTINE. Don't I?

(Thunder and lightning.)

PEGGY SUE. He was here a little while ago. *(Crossing to above*

the table SR.) The French door's open. I wonder if he went outside?
     CONNIE. No, Roy did. *(Rising.)* I'd better find him before it starts to rain and he gets soaked. *(Crossing to the French doors.)* I don't think they make drip dry tuxedos, do they? Excuse me.

(She exits SR.)

     JUSTINE. *(Rising and crossing to PEGGY SUE.)* So you've made yourself "fresh as a daisy" and are looking for "Eddie honey." Just how "personal" a secretary are you, Peggy Sue?
     PEGGY SUE. I don't have the foggiest notion what you mean.
     JUSTINE. Oh, I think you do. It seems to me you're setting yourself up to be the third Mrs. Worthington the third.
     PEGGY SUE. What Edward and I do is none of your business.
     JUSTINE. Maybe, and maybe not. If "Eddie honey" divorces Allegra and marries you, he might decide two ex-wives are more than he wants to support. I was going to ask Lawrence, here, if that mysterious envelope contains a pre-nuptial agreement for you to sign, but he says he doesn't know what's in it.
     PEGGY SUE. *(To LAWRENCE.)* You don't?
     LAWRENCE. Your guess is as good as mine, my dear.
     PEGGY SUE. A pre-nuptial agreement .... I hadn't thought it could be that. Golly, I hope so! I'm gonna find him and make him open his gifts right now!

(She hurries out UC and off UL.)

     JUSTINE. I guess I just made her day. Darn!
     DEBRA. It just occurred to me that Peggy Sue could be my next step-mother.
     LAWRENCE. *(Tongue in cheek.)* Look on the bright side, Debra — if you moved back home, Peggy Sue could cook you grits for breakfast.
     DEBRA. I'd rather eat gravel! ... and I'd rather die than live under this roof with Father again!

(EDITH enters UL.)

EDITH. Excuse me. Mrs. Vickers had me serve coffee in the parlor if any of you want some.

LAWRENCE. *(Rising.)* That sounds good. Ladies?

DEBRA. *(Rising.)* I'd like a cup.

JUSTINE. Why not? *(Crossing to UL.)* I might need the caffeine for energy if I get into a fight before this shindig is over.

DEBRA. Mom ....

JUSTINE. Just kidding, dear ... maybe ....

(LAWRENCE, DEBRA and JUSTINE exit UL. EDITH crosses to the fireplace and stares into the coals, unhappy. TONY enters UL, carrying a cup of coffee.)

TONY. I was wondering when I'd catch you alone.

EDITH. *(Startled.)* Oh! Mr. Blackwell ....

TONY. It's "Tony."

EDITH. Mrs. Vickers said ....

TONY. *(Cutting in.)* Never mind what that old dragon told you. She's not around. *(Crossing to her and putting his cup on the mantle.)* You look worried, Edith. What's the matter?

EDITH. It's ... it's Miss Beatrice.

(He takes her hand and leads her to the sofa where they sit.)

TONY. Beatrice? You mean Miss Looney Tunes?

EDITH. Don't say that! She just gets a little confused sometimes.

TONY. Sorry. I meant it in the nicest way. Tell me about her.

EDITH. Miss Beatrice's behavior has become very odd lately.

TONY. Lately?

EDITH. More than usual. She's started taking things around the house.

TONY. Things? What kind of things?

EDITH. Mostly little decorative items like, oh, a crystal ashtray, a Faberge egg ....

TONY. Faberge? We're not talking cheap trinkets, here.

EDITH. I know. Some of the objects are very valuable.

TONY. What does Beatrice do with them? Sell them?

EDITH. Oh, no! She hides them to take out and look at later, except she tends to forget where she puts them. We — the servants — are always finding things stuck away in the strangest places. We put them back where they belong.

TONY. There's no harm done, then. What are you worried about?

EDITH. We're afraid Mr. Worthington might have noticed that expensive items have been missing, and might think one of us on the staff is stealing them. Those papers he had the lawyer bring tonight — they could be our dismissal papers: mine, Ina's, Hollister's and Mrs. Vickers'.

TONY. So? If they are, you can tell him you're all innocent, that his sister has the sticky fingers.

EDITH. *(Rising.)* No! He'd have her put away! *(Crossing to DR.)* Don't you see, that's what we've been afraid of all along. We all care for Miss Beatrice a great deal. If we weren't here to protect her ....

(She starts to cry.)

TONY. *(Rising.)* She probably would have been sent to a funny farm a long time ago. *(Crossing to her.)* There, there, Edith. Don't cry. I can't stand to see a woman cry. It makes me want to take her in my arms, like this ...*(He takes EDITH into his arms.)* ... and kiss away the tears, like this...

(He starts to kiss her cheeks.)

EDITH. Oh, Tony ....
TONY. Shuuu ....

(He kisses her. After a beat, she breaks away and crosses to DC.)

EDITH. You mustn't ... I mustn't ....

TONY. There's a strong attraction between us, Edith. You feel it, too. There's no need to fight it.

EDITH. I can't ... I'd be dismissed ....

TONY. *(Crossing to her.)* Edward doesn't have to know, and what he doesn't know won't hurt us.

EDITH. Oh, Tony ....
TONY. Everything will be fine, my sweet. Just trust me.

(He starts to embrace her. MRS. VICKERS enters UL.)

MRS. VICKERS. Edith!
EDITH. *(Startled, stepping back from TONY.)* Oh!
MRS. VICKERS. That bunch in there is slurping up coffee like camels at a watering hole. We'll need another pot. Tell Ina.
EDITH. Yes, m'am.

(She hurries out UC and off UL.)

MRS. VICKERS. If you have an urge for something sweet, Mr. Blackwell, we'll be serving birthday cake shortly.
TONY. I beg your pardon?
MRS. VICKERS. You know exactly what I mean. Edith is a nice girl. I intend to see she stays that way.
TONY. *(Crossing to UC.)* Is that a threat?
MRS. VICKERS. Take it any way you like. *(Crossing to him.)* If I see you near Edith again, I'll tell Mr. Worthington what you're up to. You know as well as I how he feels about you. It won't take much to have him throw you out on your ear.
TONY. *(Angry.)* Why, you ...!
MRS. VICKERS. *(Cutting in.)* Save your breath, you two-bit gigolo! Edith is off-limits. You've been warned!

(She exits UC and off UL.)

TONY. *(Sputtering with anger.)* That ... that ... witch!
ALLEGRA. *(Entering UL.)* I trust you're not referring to me, brother, dear.
TONY. No. It's that housekeeper, Mrs. Vickers.
ALLEGRA. Ah ... did she catch you trying to raid the pantry?
TONY. I was just talking with the maid.
ALLEGRA. Uh-huh. *(Crossing to him UC.)* I told you to leave her alone. Mrs. Vickers is very protective toward Edith.

TONY. So I found out.

(He crosses to the fireplace where he gets his cup from the mantle.)

ALLEGRA. Forget about the girl, we've got bigger worries.
TONY. Such as?
ALLEGRA. *(Crossing to UR.)* That document or whatever it is Edward is carrying around.
TONY. What about it?
ALLEGRA. *(Turning back to him.)* It could be our eviction notice.
TONY. What do you mean?
ALLEGRA. I mean, they could be divorce papers. If I'm left out in the cold, you would be too, Tony. We'd both be penniless.
TONY. *(Putting his cup on the mantle.)* Divorce? Are things that bad between you?
ALLEGRA. Edward has grown tired of me, and I suspect he's already picked my replacement. At first I thought he was simply having a mild flirtation with that Dixie Creme donut, Peggy Sue. Now I'm not so sure.
TONY. Peggy Sue? *(Crossing to her.)* She's a knockout, but you're more sophisticated that she is, more glamorous than she is ....
ALLEGRA. *(Cutting in.)* Twenty years older than she is. That hominy-fed hussy has one thing I don't, Tony — youth — and that's one thing Edward's money can't buy me.
TONY. Edward's money — it should be your money, too! If he hadn't made you sign that agreement ....
ALLEGRA. But he did. I'm afraid the only way his fortune could possibly become mine is if he were to drop dead before he divorced me.
TONY. There's not much chance of that. Edward is as healthy as a horse.
ALLEGRA. Well, even horses have accidents ....
TONY. Allegra! What are you suggesting?
ALLEGRA. Nothing, Tony, nothing at all.

(Thunder and lightning. HOLLISTER enters UC from off UL.)

HOLLISTER. Excuse me, Mrs. Worthington, Mr. Blackwell.

ALLEGRA. Yes, Hollister, what is it?

HOLLISTER. Ina is bringing the birthday cake. We thought we'd gather everyone in here where Mr. Worthington can cut it and open his gifts.

ALLEGRA. Very good, Hollister. Where is Edward?

HOLLISTER. I don't know, madam. I haven't seen him since dinner.

TONY. Neither have we.

ALLEGRA. I'll look for him upstairs. Why don't you tell the others to come in here, Tony.

TONY. Alright.

ALLEGRA. Get everything prepared, Hollister. We'll be right back.

HOLLISTER. As you wish, madam.

(ALLEGRA crosses to the stairs, ascends them, and exits.)

TONY. *(As he crosses to UL.)* Oh, you'd better have a towel handy, Hollister — before this party is over, someone might be crying their eyes out.

HOLLISTER. I'll keep that in mind, sir. *(TONY exits UL; muttering to himself.)* If there's any justice, it will be you.

(INA, EDITH and MRS. VICKERS enter UC from off UL. INA carries a beautifully decorated birthday cake and EDITH carries a tray with saucers, forks, napkins, a cake server and a large knife. MRS. VICKERS smoothes the cloth on the table SR.)

MRS. VICKERS. Set the cake here, Ina

(INA sets the cake on the table SR; EDITH sets her tray beside it.)

EDITH. The cake looks beautiful, Ina.

INA. It's too good for the likes of Mr. Worthington, but thank you, Edith.

HOLLISTER. Watch what you say, Ina. You never know who

might be listening.

INA. If someone snitches to that cold-hearted monster, let 'em! I'd have quit long ago if it weren't for Miss Beatrice.

HOLLISTER. We all would have, but we have to hold our tongues for her sake.

MRS. VICKERS. She'd be lost without us.

EDITH. Yes ....

INA. I know, but he makes me so mad sometimes. At dinner, he even had the nerve to say my whipped potatoes tasted a little odd.

(The others give an almost imperceptible shudder.)

EDITH. He did compliment the gravy, though — said it was nice and thick.

INA. He was just trying to get on my good side. He knew he had made me angry. One of these days I'll carve him up along with the roast beef!

EDITH. *(Startled.)* Oh, Ina!

HOLLISTER. That's quite enough. Mr. Worthington left instructions that champagne is to be served with the cake. Ina, Edith, come with me.

(They exit UC and off UL. MRS. VICKERS adjusts the items on the table, then mutters to herself:)

MRS. VICKERS. I'd better check the downstairs bathrooms for fresh hand towels.

(She exits UC and off UL. A flash of lightning silhouettes a man outside the French doors, followed by thunder. He enters. It is EDWARD.)

EDWARD. *(To himself as he crosses to above the table SR.)* Well, well, my little envelope has created quite a stir, just as I figured it would. It seems everyone under this roof has a lot to answer for, and they will, before the night is over.

(Thunder and lightning. At last, the rain lets go and begins to pound

heavily. ROY and CONNIE rush in at the French doors SR.)

CONNIE. We just made it! I told you the rain wouldn't hold off much longer. Oh, Edward ... Roy went out for some fresh air — I had to find him.
EDWARD. *(Sarcastic.)* And you did? Will miracles never cease?
CONNIE. *(Laughing.)* Oh, you're teasing. It wasn't easy, though, you have such a large estate.
EDWARD. Which, fortunately, I can afford ... can't I, Roy? I mean, my investments are sound, aren't they?
ROY. Of course, Edward. Why do you ask?
EDWARD. I haven't examined the books for quite a while. *(Crossing to CS.)* I think it's time I went over them with you ... *(Turning back to him.)* ... say, next week?
ROY. *(Nervous.)* If you wish. I'll schedule some time Friday afternoon.
EDWARD. *(Giving him a steady look.)* Monday. Nine o'clock. Sharp.

(Thunder and lightning.)

ROY. *(Very nervous.)* Whatever you say.

(TONY, JUSTINE, DEBRA and LAWRENCE enter UL, ad-libbing about the storm. It will continue to rage.)

EDWARD. It's party time! Be seated, everyone.

(They sit thusly: ROY - US at the table SR; CONNIE - SR at the table SR; LAWRENCE - chair UR; JUSTINE, DEBRA - sofa; TONY - bench. As they do this, PEGGY SUE enters UC from off UL.)

PEGGY SUE. My goodness, Edward, I thought you had disappeared into thin air. Where on earth have you been?
EDWARD. Here and there. Have a seat, Peggy Sue.
PEGGY SUE. Don't mind if I do, sugar.

(She sits on the chair DR of the sofa. HOLLISTER enters UC from off UL followed by INA, carrying a bottle of champagne in an ice bucket, and EDITH, carrying a tray of champagne classes.)

HOLLISTER. Place them on the table with the cake.

(They do this. MRS. VICKERS enters UC from off UL with BEA-TRICE, who carries a cup of tea.)

EDWARD. Remain with us, please. I wouldn't dream of leaving you servants out of the festivities.
HOLLISTER. Yes, Mr. Worthington.

(He gestures UL. He, INA, EDITH and MRS. VICKERS stand above the sofa. BEATRICE sits on the SR end of the sofa. ALLEGRA enters UC, descending the stairs and coming into the room.)

EDWARD. *(Mockingly.)* And last to arrive, but not least, is my loving wife, Allegra. Come in, Allegra. Sit. *(He holds the chair DS of the table SR for her. She sits. EDWARD will circle the table clockwise.)* The moment you've all been anxiously awaiting has arrived! Now, let's see ... what should I do first? Cut the cake or open the gifts? *(The others, except LAWRENCE, ad-lib anxiously to open the gifts. LAWRENCE watches the proceedings calmly.)* The gifts? Are you sure? The cake looks delicious. You've outdone yourself, Ina.

(He is SL of the table.)

INA. *(Flatly.)* Glad you like it.
EDWARD. *(Picking up the cake knife.)* I don't know if I can resist it till later. Ina did work hard to make it in my honor. What kind of cake is it, Ina?
INA. Devil's food.

(EDWARD chuckles. Thunder and lightning.)

BEATRICE. Oh! I'm frightened!

EDWARD. *(Looking around the room.)* I suspect you're not the only one.

ALLEGRA. For heaven's sake, Edward, stop toying with us! You know no one cares about the cake or champagne or the stupid gifts! Tell us what's in the envelope!

EDWARD. So you prefer cutting to the chase to cutting the cake, do you, my dear? Very well. *(He lays the knife on the table.)* Since you're so consumed with curiosity to know, I'll get on with it. *(He takes the envelope from his inside coat pocket.)* A harmless-looking piece of paper, isn't it? ... but what a commotion it has caused!

JUSTINE. Of course it has, Edward. You're holding someone's fate in your hand.

DEBRA. More than one person's, possibly.

EDWARD. How right you are, daughter, how right you are.

TONY. Tell us whose, Edward!

PEGGY SUE. We're all dying to know what's in the envelope!

ROY. Get on with it!

ALLEGRA. Please ...!

EDWARD. If you insist. *(He extends the envelope to ALLEGRA.)* I'll let you do the honors, my dear. *(She rises slowly and takes it with great trepidation. He picks up the knife and holds it toward her.)* Open it.

(ALLEGRA takes it and slashes the envelope. She lays the knife on the table. She takes several folded sheets of paper from the envelope and lays the envelope on the table. She unfolds the papers and gasps. She leafs through the pages.)

ALLEGRA. They're blank! *(There is an astonished reaction from everyone, some coming to their feet.)* Is this your idea of a joke!?!

EDWARD. Not at all. *(To everyone standing.)* Sit down! *(They do. He will move about the room at will.)* I've suspected for some time that some, if not all, of you have been keeping secrets from me, perhaps even plotting and scheming to do me harm. The hostility I feel in this room is so thick you could cut it with that knife! I figured it was time to get everything out into the open, and I have. How did I accomplish this? With a little party game I devised. Let's call it "the envelope game." By making you think there were papers inside that could expose your deceitful nature, each of you projected your worst fears onto the envelope ... and discussed them amongst yourselves. All I had to do was stay out of sight and listen. They all came tumbling out, your little secrets, and I heard them: Roy's private investment, using my money; Tony's philandering; Debra's failing grades; Justine's fear that I'll cut off her support; Beatrice's kleptomania, which my faithful servants have helped cover up. I even learned, inadvertently, thanks to a comment Beatrice made, the main secret I set out to discover, namely the identity of the one among you who has been quietly selling information to a Paul Jamison. That's the man who has announced he's writing one of those malicious tell-all biographies about me. I believe the Bar Association frowns upon such unethical behavior, Lawrence.

LAWRENCE. *(Shocked, jumping up.)* What!?! I ...

EDWARD. *(Cutting in.)* Sit down! *(LAWRENCE sits.)* I'll deal with you later. *(To all.)* To conclude my litany of your offenses, there's my devoted wife, Allegra, who told her brother she would like to see me dead.

ALLEGRA. I didn't! You misunderstood me, Edward!

EDWARD. Oh, I understood perfectly. It seems the only one among you I can trust is Peggy Sue, my future bride.

(Everyone reacts.)

PEGGY SUE. *(Thrilled.)* Oh, Edward ...!

EDWARD. She's marrying me for my wealth, but at least she's honest enough to admit it.

PEGGY SUE. Not just for the money, honey-bunny — I love you too.

EDWARD. I believe you ... almost ....

(At this point, he is CS.)

JUSTINE. So what do we do now, Edward?

EDWARD. Peggy Sue and I are leaving. I've arranged a weekend get-away for us at a cozy little inn. When I return, I expect all of you to be gone. I want each and every one of you out of this house. Shortly, you'll all be out of my life — forever!

(Thunder and lightning. The lights go out. All ad-lib excitedly. They move about in the darkness. CONNIE picks up the stack of napkins from the tray; under it is a knife handle with a small, curved fish hook attached. ROY takes the handle, which matches the one on the cake knife, as CONNIE picks up the knife and puts it under the napkins, hiding it, ROY steps behind EDWARD and hooks the handle onto his coat at the center of his back. He steps back US of the table SR. During this, EDWARD takes a capsule of stage blood from his pocket and puts it into his mouth. The lightning must NOT flash during this stage business. As this happens:)

DEBRA. The lights!
CONNIE. Oh, dear!
PEGGY SUE. It must be the storm.
TONY. Ow! My foot!
JUSTINE. Sorry 'bout that.
HOLLISTER. Everyone, please remain calm. There is a generator for just such an occurrence. It will activate automatically any moment now. *(The lights come back on.)* There, you see?
CONNIE. I do, now.

(EDITH looks at EDWARD's back and screams. He has a stunned expression on his face. He groans. Blood begins to come from the corner of his mouth. The others react, shocked. EDWARD points a finger at ALLEGRA, then begins a slow turn in place clockwise, the pointing finger moving over all of the others, until he's completed the circle. As he revolves, the knife in his back becomes visible to the audience. He crumples to the floor, dead, his head pointing DS. The others are all standing. The SERVANTS have moved to UC near the archway. BEATRICE is above the SR end of the sofa. HOLLISTER takes her arm to support her. DEBRA and JUSTINE are below the sofa. TONY is SL of PEGGY SUE at her chair. CONNIE is SR of ALLEGRA, below her chair.

LAWRENCE is US of the table SR, with ROY. LAWRENCE rushes to EDWARD, kneels, and lifts one hand at the wrist, feeling for a pulse.)

LAWRENCE. *(After a beat.)* He's dead.

(Thunder and lightning. He lets the hand fall to the floor.)

PEGGY SUE. Oh ....

(She faints, falling into the arms of TONY who catches her.)

EDWARD. *(As WALTER.)* Freeze! *(Everyone freezes, creating a tableau of shocked murder suspects. The storm halts. EDWARD/ WALTER raises the upper half of his body up, pushing with his hands, and looks at the audience.)* Wasn't that exciting? *(He licks the blood at his mouth with his tongue, then smacks his lips.)* Kayro corn syrup and red food coloring. Whew! I'll probably get a sugar rush like you wouldn't believe! As I'm sure you've guessed, this is the conclusion of Act One. You might have noticed I did delay the rain. You're welcome. At any rate, it's time for the intermission, so you can stretch your legs and do...whatever you need to do. See you in fifteen minutes.

(He flops back down into his dead position. The others break their freeze, ad-libbing wildly, except CONNIE who scratches both arms like crazy. Rain, thunder and lightning. The lights fade out as the curtain closes. Somber music fades in and plays during intermission.)

INTERMISSION

ACT II

*(The music fades out as the curtain opens and the stage lights fade
up. It is several hours later. The storm has passed, leaving darkness outside the French doors. The cake, champagne and other
items on the table SR have been struck, including the envelope
and papers. The cast is seen thusly: LAWRENCE - chair UR;
ROY - US of table SR; CONNIE - SR of table SR; ALLEGRA - DS
of table SR; JUSTINE, DEBRA, BEATRICE - sofa; TONY -
bench; PEGGY SUE - chair DR of sofa; INA, HOLLISTER, MRS.
VICKERS and EDITH stand behind the sofa. Everyone except
PEGGY SUE holds their hands at chest level, palms out; all have
ink on their fingertips from being fingerprinted. There is a tape
outline on the floor, CS, where EDWARD lay after he died. During the act, everyone will step over the outline as if it were the
body itself. The effect will be comical if each person seems un-
conscious of the fact that they are taking a big step when they
cross it. Standing DS of the outline, his back to the audience, is
LT. JAMES McMILLAN, a police detective. He wears an open
trench coat over a suit and tie, and a fedora hat. He is holding a
pad and pen.)*

JAMES. So Edward Worthington the third is dead, and one of
you killed him .... *(He turns toward the audience. We see that JAMES
is being played by WALTER. He has removed the glasses and silver in
his hair, and is now wearing a moustache as well as the different
clothes. As WALTER.)* Welcome back. It's me — Walter. *(Moving at
will.)* Act One came easily enough, but Act Two — Act Two is the
tricky one. A murder has been committed; now it must be solved. In

some of my mysteries, I isolate the characters, say on an island or mountain top or in the woods during a blizzard. The murderer cuts the phone lines, trapping everyone there with him or her. In this type of situation, the murder is usually solved by an amateur sleuth among them, a Miss Marple or Jessica Fletcher wannabe, for example. At other times, such as this one, I bring in a homicide detective to catch the culprit. I'll be playing just such a character, Lt. James McMillan. Well, I can't sit back and let them ... *(Indicating the others.)* ... do all the work, can I? If you've been taking notes on "how to commit a murder," you should have written down that you must provide your suspects with motives and an opportunity to do in the victim. Everyone in this play had a motive to kill Edward except Peggy Sue who stood to gain access to a fortune had he lived ....

    PEGGY SUE. *(To the audience.)* I have rotten luck.

    ALLEGRA. *(To PEGGY SUE.)* Not as rotten as Edward's.

    JAMES. Ah-hum. *(Clearing his throat to get their attention.)* As I was saying, all but Miss Dixie Cup had a motive, and they all had the opportunity to stab the man in the back — literally. In case you're curious how we created that great special effect, during the blackout Connie hid the cake knife under the pile of napkins on the table while Roy took a matching knife handle with a hook attached from there and stuck it to Edward's coat. Edward slipped a blood capsule from his pocket into his mouth and bit down. Simple, huh? But I digress.... In Act Two, Lt. McMillan — I — will search for clues, question the suspects, and by its conclusion, discover who murdered Edward Worthington the third. Keep your eyes and ears open. Who knows? You might guess the killer's identity before I do! Now, on with the show.... *(He goes back into character. By this point he is DL.)* You've all told me, as a group, what happened. At this point, I intend to question each of you again, individually. I'll start with you, Miss Brumley.

    ALLEGRA. *(Rising.)* Thank goodness. I, for one, am anxious to wash my hands.

    MRS. VICKERS. Everyone should, before they get ink all over the furniture. Miss Beatrice has already finger-painted the coffee table top.

    BEATRICE. Clumsy me ....

    HOLLISTER. Don't fret, Miss Beatrice. Mrs. Vickers will clean it for you.

CONNIE. *(Rising.)* I've been dying to scratch .. hives ... nerves ....

JAMES. I regret the inconvenience, but it's standard procedure to fingerprint all the suspects at the crime scene.

ALLEGRA. If we're excused, I'm going to my suite to cleanse my digits.

HOLLISTER. May I suggest the guests gather in the parlor next door? There's a half-bath across the hall. The staff can wait in the kitchen until you're ready for us.

JAMES. That's a good idea.

(Everyone who's still seated, except PEGGY SUE, rises. The SER-VANTS exit UC and off UL. ALLEGRA ascends the stairs and exits. CONNIE, ROY, BEATRICE, LAWRENCE, JUSTINE, TONY and DEBRA exit UL. Everyone holds their hands out comically, careful not to touch anything. Everyone will wash the ink off their fingers.)

PEGGY SUE. What would you like to know, lieutenant?

JAMES. *(Flipping through the pages in his pad.)* Let's see, Miss Brumley, you said you were Mr. Worthington's personal secretary. How long have you served in that capacity?

PEGGY SUE. About six months, I guess. I mean, I've worked for Worthington Enterprises for a couple of years, but when Edward's personal assistant retired last June, he pulled me from the secretarial pool and gave me her job.

JAMES. Obviously, your relationship became very personal if he announced his intention tonight to marry you.

PEGGY SUE. What can I say? It happens. *(Rising.)* I would have made Edward a good wife, lieutenant ... better than that ice cube he was married to. *(Crossing to DR.)* Allegra can shoot you a look that would give you frostbite. *(Turning back to him.)* If I had to guess, I'd say she's your murderer, Lt. McMillan.

JAMES. *(Sitting on the bench SL.)* Possibly, but it's been my experience that a jilted spouse often strikes out at the competition, in this case, you.

PEGGY SUE. You mean you think she would have gone after me with that pig-sticker? Golly! The very idea gives me the shivers.

(She hugs herself and shivers.)

JAMES. Mrs. Worthington might well have killed her husband. I'm just saying there are other possibilities.

PEGGY SUE. I have to admit you're right. *(She will cross to above the sofa, stepping over the outline.)* I'd rather stitch my lips shut with a sewing machine than say something bad about anybody, but Allegra's brother, Tony, could have done it for her. He's a charmer, but I wouldn't trust him any further than I could throw a pig-skin with the pig still in it! And Roy and Lawrence had good reasons to kill Edward, too — he was going to fire both of them. Eddie threatened to bring criminal charges against Roy, as well as to report Lawrence's dealings with that writer Jamison to the Bar Association.

JAMES. So I noted. His sister, ex-wife and daughter and servants had motives to end his life as well. Mrs. Phillips might have committed the crime to protect her husband. If there's anything worse than having no suspects in a murder case, it's having too many. Apparently you are the only one in the house who stood to lose, not gain, by Mr. Worthington's death. You're the only one I feel sure didn't stab the man.

PEGGY SUE. Thanks ever so much. Then can I go home now? *(Crossing to UR.)* I'm about to absolutely collapse from exhaustion, but before I do anything else, I have to look over the classified ads.

JAMES. The classifieds?

PEGGY SUE. *(Turning back.)* Why, yes, lieutenant. When I lost Edward, I lost my job. If Allegra is going to take charge of Worthington Enterprises, you can bet your boots the first thing she'll do is give me the ax. *(She shivers.)* Ooooo ... I wish I hadn't said it like that. I gave myself the shivers again. A goose just walked over my grave.

JAMES. I beg your pardon?

PEGGY SUE. That's what we say in the South when we get the shivers — "A goose just walked over my grave."

JAMES. It's a quaint expression, though I can't see how anyone would link poultry with the hereafter. I gather it's used to express a feeling of impending doom.

PEGGY SUE. I guess so. In that case, I bet a whole flock of geese stomped over Edward's cemetery plot a few hours ago. Anyway, can I leave, Lt. McMillan?

JAMES. *(Rising.)* Not yet. I might have more questions for you after I talk with the others. Sorry.

PEGGY SUE. That's okay. I'm happy to do whatever I can to help. *(Crossing to UL.)* I'll be in the parlor if you need me.

(She exits UL. JAMES takes a cell phone from his coat pocket, punches in a number, then puts it to his ear, crossing DR.)

JAMES. Pete? McMillan here. How are the fingerprints coming? … That's it? The only ones on the handle that weren't smudged were the victim's and his wife's? … Too bad; everyone saw him give her the knife to open an envelope ....What!?! You found traces of what!?! … That could be a vital clue! Excellent work, Pete! … Yeah … there's only one suspect who logically could have left it there, but if someone else ....'Fraid not — they've all been fingerprinted, as you know, and are washing their hands now....Yeah .... Too bad. There goes the evidence, right down the drain. I'll have to find out another way. If I'm going to discover who murdered Edward Worthington, I've got my work cut out for me.... No, that wasn't meant to be a pun. … Uh-huh ....Thanks again, Pete. I'll check you later.

(He punches the off button and puts the phone back into his coat pocket. He crosses to the archway, stepping over the outline, and pulls the bell cord, then crosses to UR, thinking. After a couple of beats, EDITH enters at the archway from off UL.)

EDITH. You rang, sir?
JAMES. Yes … Edith, isn't it?
EDITH. Yes, sir.
JAMES. Would you ask the other servants to come in, please, as well as yourself?
EDITH. Of course, Lt. McMillan.

(She exits off UL. JAMES looks through his notes. After a few beats, EDITH, INA, HOLLISTER and MRS. VICKERS ENTER UC from off UL.)

HOLLISTER. You wish to see us, sir?

JAMES. I do. Be seated, please. *(They sit at the table SR: MRS. VICKERS - DS; HOLLISTER - US; EDITH - SR; INA - SL. JAMES will move about at will, taking notes.)* I have a few more questions concerning what took place tonight.

HOLLISTER. I don't know how we can help you, lieutenant. We were in the kitchen most of the evening.

JAMES. It's what took place in the kitchen that I need to know about at this point. I'm specifically interested in finding out about the murder weapon, the knife.

INA. My knife? What about my knife?

JAMES. Where is it usually kept?

INA. In a butcher block. It's part of a set.

MRS. VICKERS. It's seldom there, though. It's Ina's favorite kitchen tool.

INA. That's true. I use it to slice and dice everything ... not including people, if that's what you're thinking.

JAMES. I'm not thinking anything, at the moment.

INA. A good, sharp knife is hard to come by. I'd like to have it back when the case is closed ... or is that too morbid?

MRS. VICKERS, HOLLISTER & EDITH. That's too morbid.

JAMES. I assume you used the knife while preparing dinner?

INA. Naturally. I chopped up some fresh chives to sprinkle on the whipped potatoes.

(Everyone gives an almost imperceptible shudder.)

JAMES. What else was served?

INA. Roast beef, gravy, Brussels sprouts ....

JAMES. A salad?

INA. Congealed. Jello and fruit.

JAMES. *(An aside to the audience, as WALTER.)* At first I considered titling the play "The Blood, Like Jello, Congeals," but then I thought, "Naw, that's pretty gross." I wouldn't want to go see a play with that title, would you? *(Back into character.)* So you didn't prepare a salad dressing, say, oil and vinegar?

INA. No, sir.

MRS. VICKERS. Mr. Worthington couldn't stand lettuce.

EDITH. I heard him say once if he had been meant to eat green, leafy things, he would have been born a rabbit.

JAMES. I see. What did you do with the knife after the meal was prepared, Ina?

INA. Washed it, of course, along with all the other utensils. In the dishwasher.

JAMES. Who touched it after that?

EDITH. I did. Ina told me to take it out of the dishwasher and put it on the tray with the saucers and forks and things for the birthday cake. It was still damp, so I wiped it off good with a dish towel.

JAMES. And nobody else touched it? There were no fingerprints except possibly yours, or traces of food on it when you brought the knife in here?

EDITH. No, sir. It wasn't out of my sight the whole time.

JAMES. That's what I needed to know. You've all been very helpful.

HOLLISTER. If it's a matter of any of our fingerprints being on the knife...

JAMES. *(Cutting in.)* It isn't that ... uh ... Hollister. The only discernible prints on the weapon belong to Mr. and Mrs. Worthington whom we know touched it.

HOLLISTER. I see ....

MRS. VICKERS. Then how have we helped?

JAMES. I'll explain later ... I hope.... For now, I need to take a quick look around the kitchen, if I may.

HOLLISTER. *(Rising.)* As you wish. This way, Lt. McMillan.

(EDITH, MRS. VICKERS and INA rise. ALL cross to the archway UC and exit off UL except EDITH. As she starts to follow the others out, TONY enters UL, stealthily.)

TONY. Pssst! Edith!

EDITH. Tony! What are you doing here?
TONY. Close the doors.

(EDITH slides the doors UC shut.)

EDITH. Were you eavesdropping on us?
TONY. Of course not. I just happened to be listening in this direction. *(Crossing to her.)* So the murderer didn't leave any prints on the knife ....
EDITH. Unless it was Mrs. Worthington.
TONY. Sis? It wasn't her.
EDITH. How can you be sure?
TONY. For one thing, Edward was stabbed in the back. Allegra was sitting in front of him. If she had grabbed the knife off the table and stuck him with it, she would have hit him in the chest.
EDITH. Maybe, but it was too dark to see. Mr. Worthington could have turned around to start toward the light switch.

(She touches the switch by the archway.)

TONY. Clever girl, as well as pretty. *(Embracing her.)* I knew you were special from the first time I laid eyes on you.
EDITH. You shouldn't ....
TONY. I know; that's what makes it so much fun. *(He kisses her.)* Let's slip outside where we can be alone.
EDITH. Lt. McMillan will want to question you, too.
TONY. Not for a while. He's busy in the kitchen with Betty Crocker, Lurch, and the Happy Homemaker. Come on.

(He takes her hand and pulls her to the French doors.)

EDITH. But, it's cold out there....
TONY. Don't worry — I'll keep you warm.

(They exit SR, leaving one door ajar. After a beat, ROY enters UL followed by CONNIE.)

ROY. *(Nervous.)* He thinks I did it! I know that policeman thinks

I killed Edward!

CONNIE. Why would he, Roy? Why should he suspect you any more than the rest of us?

ROY. I could tell he doesn't believe I put that money in my account on Edward's behalf.

CONNIE. Why not? I believe you.

ROY. That doesn't count — you're my wife.

CONNIE. I think it counts. A wife should do anything she can to help her husband.

ROY. *(Suspicious.)* Even … commit murder?

CONNIE. You think I murdered Edward? *(She gives a giddy laugh.)* That's silly! You know how klutzy I am, Roy. If I had tried to grab a knife in the dark, I probably would have cut a pinkie off!

(She laughs again.)

ROY. That's true … if not yours, somebody else's. *(Looking around as he crosses to DC, stepping over the outline.)* Where's the lieutenant? I want to volunteer to be questioned next and get it over with. My nerves are shot.

CONNIE. When I came out of that half-bath across the hall a few minutes ago, I saw him going toward the kitchen with the servants.

ROY. Oh. I meant to ask you, what were you doing in there so long?

CONNIE. *(Crossing to him, stepping over the outline.)* Checking the medicine cabinet for calamine lotion. I didn't find any, but that's okay — the itching has stopped.

ROY. Good.

CONNIE. I'm getting better, honey. Before tonight, I hadn't broken out in hives for so long the scratches on my arms healed up.

ROY. I noticed. It was nice having a wife who didn't look like an inept lion tamer for a change.

CONNIE. I was thinking about buying some short sleeve dresses, but I guess that's out, now.

ROY. I'd say so. Connie, did you notice any aspirin in that medicine cabinet? I've got one of my splitting headaches.

CONNIE. No, dear, I'm afraid I didn't. I'll bet Allegra keeps some in the guest suite. I'll run up and look.

ROY. I had better go with you. With your sense of direction, you could end up in the neighbor's bathroom.

CONNIE. *(Giggling.)* Oh, Roy .... *(They cross to the doors UC, stepping over the outline.)* Poor Edward ... he didn't even get to open his presents. I think he would have liked the sweater we got him.

ROY. Maybe you can return it to Wal-Mart for a refund.

(He slides open the doors UC. MRS. VICKERS is standing there. ROY and CONNIE jump, startled.)

MRS. VICKERS. Have you seen Edith?
ROY. No, we haven't. Excuse us.

(He and CONNIE go past her, ascend the stairs, and exit. MRS. VICKERS looks around the room and notices the French door that's ajar.)

MRS. VICKERS. Uh-huh ....

(She crosses to the French doors and exits. A beat later, BEATRICE enters at the archway from off UL. She is carrying a large vase, awkwardly, her manner furtive. She looks around, then ascends the stairs and exits. JUSTINE and DEBRA enter UL. DEBRA is carrying a large flower arrangement.)

JUSTINE. There's got to be something in here to put them in. They were on the hall table?

DEBRA. Next to the half-bath. I'm sure the flowers were in a container when I went in. When I came out, they were lying there in a clump.

JUSTINE. *(At the table UL.)* Here's a vase. You can put them in it.

DEBRA. Alright. *(Looking in the vase.)* There's something inside.

JUSTINE. What?

DEBRA. They look like colored pebbles.

JUSTINE. No problem. *(She takes the flowers from DEBRA and jambs them into the vase.)* So where's the detective?

DEBRA. I don't know. Shouldn't we wait in the parlor until he's ready to question us?

JUSTINE. Why? Nobody else is. I wish whoever poked Edward would 'fess up so we could all go home, but I don't suppose that's likely to happen.

DEBRA. *(Crossing to the fireplace.)* Mom, you didn't do it, did you? Kill Father?

JUSTINE. No, dear, I can't take credit for that, though I've threatened to lots of times. I know I was always cutting him down, but I didn't do it literally.

DEBRA. *(Sitting on the bench.)* I hope you can convince Lt. McMillan of that.

JUSTINE. *(Crossing to DC, stepping over the outline, and on to DR. JUSTINE and DEBRA don't notice ALLEGRA enter, descending the stairs.)* He seems like a pretty smart guy. The lieutenant should realize that if I had been going to knock off Edward, I'd have done it years ago when he left us to marry Allegra, The Shark Woman. He'd have a hard time proving that I killed my ex in a fit of anger that lasted ten years.

ALLEGRA. *(At the archway.)* If anyone could hold a grudge that long, you could, Justine ... except you wouldn't have needed a knife. With that sharp tongue of yours, you could have licked him to death.

JUSTINE. Well, speak of the devil, and she appears! Still here? I'm surprised you didn't make the most of the opportunity and run out to buy a new black dress.

ALLEGRA. With what? *(Stepping into the room.)* You know I don't have any money of my own, and I'm sure Edward's accounts will be frozen for quite some time.

JUSTINE. Good point. Speaking of money, the fact that he was supporting Debra and me should be proof that I didn't kill him. I'm not dumb enough to slay the goose that was laying the golden eggs.

ALLEGRA. But tonight he threatened to cut off your income.

JUSTINE. I know, but he's done that for years, every time I ticked him off, which was often. If he actually did stop my alimony checks, I might consider homicide, but not until then.

(PEGGY SUE enters UL in a huff.)

PEGGY SUE. The very idea! *(Noticing the others, stopping above the sofa.)* Oh!

LAWRENCE. *(Entering UL behind her.)* Let me explain ....

PEGGY SUE. *(To the group.)* What's going on?

JUSTINE. *(Facetiously.)* A meeting of Edward's wives — past, present, and future. We were just waiting for you to join us.

DEBRA. What was going on out there?

PEGGY SUE. This snake in the grass, Lawrence, made a pass at me!

LAWRENCE. *(Reaching for her shoulder.)* Peggy Sue ....

PEGGY SUE. Keep your scaly hands to yourself! *(She crosses SL past him and around to DL; to the others.)* I told Lawrence I'll be looking for a new job, now that Edward's dead. He offered me one with his firm, and then tried to show me some of the fringe benefits! If Edward could see what you tried to do, he'd be spinning in his grave ... if he were in it yet!

DEBRA. How could Father see Lawrence if he were in his grave?

PEGGY SUE. Oh, you know what I meant!

LAWRENCE. I've felt a tremendous attraction for you for a long time, Peggy Sue, but I couldn't tell you as long as Edward ....

ALLEGRA. *(Cutting in.)* Was alive. *(To all, crossing to DC, stepping over the outline.)* Well, well, it seems that Edward's trusted lawyer had yet another motive to murder him.

JUSTINE. For once, I have to agree with you, Allegra, although it hurts me like a toothache to admit it.

LAWRENCE. No! I wouldn't kill Edward because I, too, have romantic feelings for Peggy Sue!

PEGGY SUE. It's a good thing, 'cause I wouldn't have you on a Christmas tree!

LAWRENCE. Why, because I'm not rich? That is what drew you to your boss, wasn't it — his millions?

PEGGY SUE. What if it was? I'm tired of being poor. As my grandma told me, "Love is fleeting, honey, but money lasts forever."

JUSTINE. Are you sure you're not descended from Scarlett O'Hara?

*(All turn toward the French doors as MRS. VICKERS enters pulling
    EDITH by the wrist.)*

MRS. VICKERS. That ought to teach him a lesson!
EDITH. Mrs. Vickers, you shouldn't have ....
MRS. VICKERS. He can't say I didn't warn him! *(To the others.)*
Don't mind us, we're just passing through.

(She pulls EDITH to UC.)

EDITH. But... but ....

*(MRS. VICKERS PULLS EDITH through the archway and they exit
    off UL.)*

DEBRA. Wonder what that was all about?

*(TONY enters at the French doors. A trickle of blood comes from
    each nostril.)*

TONY. I don't believe she did that ....
ALLEGRA. Tony! Your nose ....
TONY. It's nothing compared to what my eye is going to look
like.
ALLEGRA. *(Crossing to him UR, stepping over the outline.)*
Maybe next time you'll listen to me. Come on — I'll wet a towel in
the half-bath and clean it off.

*(They go through the archway and exit off UL where TONY will clean
    the blood from his nose, as BEATRICE enters, descending the
    stairs.)*

JUSTINE. *(Musing.)* Doesn't anybody use the front door? When I
lived here, we used the front door all the time.
PEGGY SUE. *(To LAWRENCE.)* You men! You're all alike!
LAWRENCE. What!?! I'm not like Tony! I was only trying to
comfort you!

PEGGY SUE. Sure you were! If you had comforted me any more, my daddy would have come after you with a shotgun!

BEATRICE. *(At the archway.)* Everyone is back in here. Are we playing a new game?

DEBRA. No, Aunt Bea, we wouldn't dream of playing a game without you.

BEATRICE. That's sweet, Debra. One of these days I'm going to surprise you and win one. *(Looking around.)* Are there any nibbles in here? I was saving room for birthday cake, so I didn't eat much dinner. Then nobody cut it.

DEBRA. *(Rising and crossing above the sofa to her.)* I noticed. You picked at your roast beef and didn't even touch your whipped potatoes.

(Everyone gives an almost imperceptible shudder.)

BEATRICE. There were some mints in here earlier. Now, where did they go to ...? *(She looks at the vase on the table UL and is surprised to see flowers in it.)* Never mind.

DEBRA. I'll get you something. *(She pulls the bell cord, then takes BEATRICE's arm.)* Come sit on the sofa, Aunt Bea.

(They cross around the sofa, stepping over the outline, and sit.)

LAWRENCE. I have to make a phone call. If you ladies will excuse me?

PEGGY SUE. Gladly!

(LAWRENCE exits UL.)

JUSTINE. *(Sitting on the DS chair of the table SR.)* If I had to guess, I'd say he's going to tell that writer the good news.

PEGGY SUE. *(Crossing to the bench and sitting.)* Good news? What good news?

JUSTINE. That Edward has gone to meet his Maker. On second thought, I doubt that's where he's headed. Anyway, Lawrence is a very lucky lawyer. Not only is the man who was going to have him disbarred dead, that Jamison guy will probably pay him a fortune for a first-hand account of Edward's murder. With a climax like that, Edward Worthington the third's biography will be a huge best seller.

PEGGY SUE. I told you Lawrence was a snake!
JUSTINE. You won't get an argument from me.

(EDITH enters at the archway from off UL.)

EDITH. Did someone ring?
DEBRA. Yes, Edith. My aunt is a little hungry. Will you see if you can find something to serve?
EDITH. Yes, Miss Debra. It might take me a minute. That police detective is searching through everything in the kitchen — the cabinets, refrigerator, everywhere. I'll do what I can.

(She exits off UL as ROY and CONNIE ENTER, descending the stairs.)

PEGGY SUE. He's searching the kitchen? Wonder what for?
BEATRICE. Maybe he's hungry, too.
ROY. You should have paid more attention to the label.
CONNIE. I'm sorry, honey. It was an accident.
ROY. Perhaps I should see a doctor.
CONNIE. I don't know what he could do. *(They are at the archway.)* Oh, hello again, everybody.
JUSTINE. What's the matter? You look a little green around the gills, Roy.
ROY. I had — still have — a ferocious headache. We couldn't find any aspirin in the guest suite bathroom, so my wife went to rummage in Allegra's medicine chest. Stupid me swallowed the pills she brought me without looking closely at them.
DEBRA. It wasn't aspirin?
CONNIE. Well, no. I didn't see any aspirin, but there was this vial of big orange pills that look like the prescription strength Motrin Roy keeps at home for his headaches. I gave him those before I read on the label that they were Premarin instead. *(To ROY.)* I only gave

you four.
DEBRA. Premarin? What's premarin?
CONNIE. Double-strength estrogen.

(JUSTINE whoops with laughter.)

JUSTINE. If Roy gets a sudden urge to try on your dresses, Connie, you'll know why!

(She whoops again.)

ROY. *(Flipping a hand at JUSTINE in a feminine manner.)* Oh, stop it!

(Horrified at what he did, ROY jambs the hand under his other arm-pit.)

CONNIE. Uh ... honey ... why don't you sit down.

(ROY crosses to the chair DR of the sofa, unaware that his walk has become comically feminine, steps over the outline, and sits. He crosses one leg over the other one at the knee and swings his foot.)

DEBRA. Connie, Edith is bringing some snacks if you'd like to join us.
CONNIE. *(Crossing to the sofa, stepping over the outline, and sitting.)* Oh, good. Maybe having something on Roy's stomach will absorb the ... you know ....

(ROY pulls at his collar with one hand while he fans his face with the other.)

ROY. It's hot in here! Why is it suddenly so hot in here!?!
JUSTINE. Trust me—it'll pass.

*(ALLEGRA and TONY enter at the archway from off UL. TONY has a

large piece of toilet paper sticking from each nostril.)
ALLEGRA. Isn't that better?
TONY. *(Nasally.)* I can't breeve.
ALLEGRA. So which had you rather do? Breathe or bleed?
TONY. I'll manage this way. I need to sit down.

*(He sits at the UC chair at the table SR. ALLEGRA crosses to the SR
chair there and sits.)*

CONNIE. What happened, Tony?
TONY. Mrs. Vickers poked me in the nose.
ROY. That mean ol' thing! If I were you, I'd scratch her eyes out!
CONNIE. I'm sorry, Allegra, but Roy took some of your Prema-
rin by mistake. I thought it was Motrin.
TONY. What's Premarin?
CONNIE. Female hormones.
ROY. Why don't you tell just everybody! *(He bursts into tears.)*
I'm sorry ... I'm sorry ... I don't know what's come over me ....

(He pulls a handkerchief from a pocket and dabs his eyes.)

BEATRICE. Oh, dear .... What's the matter with Mr. Phillips?
DEBRA. He's got in touch with his feminine side.
ALLEGRA. Actually, he's in touch with my feminine side — it
was my prescription he took.
PEGGY SUE. If you've got any pills left, can I have a few? I
want to slip some into Lawrence's drink, then see how he likes getting
pinched on the ....
BEATRICE. *(Cutting in.)* Whatever happened to topics of con-
versation I can understand, like the weather ...?
ROY. ... hairstyles ....

(JAMES enters at the archway from off UL.)

JAMES. Let's talk about murder. *(To the audience, as WALTER.)*
Look, I know I told you that I wouldn't stoop to using low humor, but
Roy and the estrogen bit got out of hand. Straighten up, Roy.

ROY. *(With a heavy sigh.)* Oh, alright.
(He assumes a more masculine posture and slides the crossed leg so that the ankle rests on the other knee.)

JAMES. And Tony, take the toilet paper out of your nose. You look like a walrus.
TONY. That's a relief.

(He removes the paper.)

JAMES. Now, then .... *(Back into character.)* Let's talk about murder.
ALLEGRA. So, Lt. McMillan, do you know who killed my husband?
JUSTINE. My ex-husband?
PEGGY SUE. My future husband?
BEATRICE. Little bubba?
JAMES. Not yet, but the head of our crime lab, Pete, passed on some interesting information that might prove to be relevant.
JUSTINE. I don't suppose you'd tell us what it is?
JAMES. When the time is right.

(HOLLISTER, MRS. VICKERS, EDITH and INA enter UC from off UL. EDITH and INA carry trays of hors d'oeuvres. In this scene, JAMES will move about at will.)

HOLLISTER. Excuse me, Lt. McMillan, Miss Debra said Miss Beatrice was hungry, and requested we bring in some food.
INA. We thought everyone else might like a snack, as well. After Mr. Worthington's announcement, no one seemed to have much of an appetite for dinner. The roast was barely eaten, and nobody touched my ... *(Slight pause as everyone gears up to shudder.)* ... Brussels sprouts.

(Everyone relaxes.)

MRS. VICKERS. There were plenty of hors d'oeuvres left as

well, so we brought them out.

BEATRICE. Oh, good ... nibbles!

HOLLISTER. *(To JAMES.)* May we?

JAMES. Certainly. *(INA puts her tray on the table SR as EDITH puts hers on the coffee table. As they do this:)* Mrs. Vickers, all of the household seems to have migrated back here to the living room except Mr. Tate. Will you find him, please, and ask him to join us?

MRS. VICKERS. Yes, lieutenant.

PEGGY SUE. The snake slithered into the parlor a few minutes ago.

(MRS. VICKERS raises an eyebrow at this, then exits UL.)

JAMES. Please, help yourselves.

(The others nibble the hors d'oeuvres. BEATRICE finds one without an olive. MRS. VICKERS and LAWRENCE enter UL.)

LAWRENCE. You wanted to see me, Lt. McMillan?

JAMES. Yes. Join us, please. *(LAWRENCE crosses to the table SR, stepping over the outline, and sits on the SL chair.)* Staff, if you will remain as well?

(HOLLISTER, MRS. VICKERS, INA and EDITH stand above the sofa.)

ROY. Lt. McMillan, I have a headache and I don't feel at all well.

JUSTINE. Something you ate, no doubt.

ROY. If you're ready to question us again, I'd like to volunteer to go first and get it over with.

JAMES. That's fine, Mr. Phillips, but I'm not going to question you, they are. *(He indicates the audience. He speaks to them as WALTER.)* As I mentioned earlier, I intended to question each of the suspects individually in this act, but my call to Pete at the crime lab furnished an important clue I had to follow up on. In order to conclude the play at a decent hour — which I'm sure you would appreciate —

we need to speed things up. Can you raise the house lights, please? *(The house lights come up.)*

*******AUDIENCE PARTICIPATION INTERROGATIONS*******

(For the next ten minutes or so, WALTER will lead the audience in interrogating the suspects. He can move about at will to each suspect as he or she is being questioned. They will stop eating and observe the action. You may choose to allow the actors to ad-lib in character in response to one another's comments.)

JAMES as WALTER. At this point, I'm going to allow you to question or accuse the suspect you believe to be the murderer. Since Mr. Phillips volunteered to go first, let's start with him. Keep in mind that the killer will no doubt lie to protect himself or herself. Will all of you in the audience who think Mr. Phillips murdered Edward Worthington please stand? *(Several in the audience should stand.)* If you have a question or comment for this suspect, raise your hand and I'll call on you in turn.

(WALTER will improvise this section, moving to the suspects in turn, having members of the audience who think each is the killer stand, and leading them in presenting their questions and comments. The suspects will respond in character. PEGGY SUE is not a suspect, but can be addressed if anyone in the audience asks to. BEATRICE will be the last to be questioned. She will nibble an hors d'oeuvre nervously during her interrogation.)

JAMES as WALTER. Thank you. Now that we have reviewed the suspects' motives and actions, let's proceed to the climax and reveal who, indeed, murdered Edward Worthington the third. House lights! *(The house lights fade out. JAMES goes back into character.)*

*******END OF INTERROGATIONS*******

JAMES. As we've learned, any of you could have killed Mr. Worthington, but only one of you did the deed. The question is, who?

(BEATRICE takes an olive slice from an hors d'oeuvre and drops it onto the floor. ALLEGRA notices this, as does JAMES.)

ALLEGRA. Beatrice, what on earth are you doing?
BEATRICE. Getting rid of those black things. I don't like 'em.
ALLEGRA. For goodness' sake, don't throw the olive slices onto the floor! I thought they were bugs!
TONY. So did I.
JAMES. Olive slices?
INA. Black olives, Lt. McMillan. I put slices of them on some of the hors d'oeuvres.
JAMES. *(To BEATRICE.)* I gather, Miss Worthington, that you removed olives from the hors d'oeuvres earlier tonight, say, before dinner?
BEATRICE. Oh, yes, lieutenant. I never eat them. They taste nasty.
JAMES. I see. Did anyone else remove the olives from your hors d'oeuvres before you ate them?

(The others who ate hors d'oeuvres ad-lib they didn't.)

JUSTINE. I confess. *(Everyone looks at her, surprised.)* I picked a pimento off one and put it on the hors d'oeuvre next to it. Really, Lt. McMillan, surely playing with one's food hasn't become a crime. Shouldn't you concentrate on solving Edward's murder?
JAMES. That's precisely what I am doing, Mrs. Worthington. In fact, I know now who the murderer is. *(Everyone reacts, surprised. To EDITH.)* Edith, you stated you wiped the cake knife with a dish towel after it had been cleaned in the dishwasher, am I correct?
EDITH. Yes, sir.
JAMES. And you said no one touched it until Mr. Worthington, and then his wife?
EDITH. That's right. But what ...?

JAMES. *(Cutting in.)* Then only one person could have left traces of the substance my lab chief found on the handle — oil ... olive oil.

MRS. VICKERS. That's what you were searching the kitchen for.

JAMES. Yes, but I was looking for bottled olive oil that you cook with.

INA. I don't use it. I prefer Crisco.

JAMES. So I noticed. It didn't occur to me to look for a jar of olives themselves. Obviously, they were the source of the oil that Miss Worthington passed from her fingers to the murder weapon.

(Everyone reacts.)

DEBRA. Oh, no...

JAMES. Miss Worthington, will you come with me, please?

(At this point, JAMES is UC.)

BEATRICE. With you? *(Rising.)* I suppose so .... *(Crossing to him.)* Where are we going, lieutenant?

JAMES. To jail. *(Taking handcuffs from his belt or handcuff pouch.)* I'm arresting you for the murder of your brother, Edward Worthington.

(Everyone reacts.)

BEATRICE. You think I killed little bubba? Well, maybe I did ... I don't remember very well ... it was so confusing in the dark ....

DEBRA. Oh, Aunt Bea...

HOLLISTER. *(Crossing to JAMES and BEATRICE.)* Wait, Lt. McMillan. Miss Beatrice didn't kill anyone. She couldn't hurt a fly. I murdered the master.

(Big reaction from everyone.)

JUSTINE. Can you believe that? The butler did it!

ALLEGRA. Good for you, Hollister. If you weren't going to the slammer, I'd give you a raise.

JAMES. Please, ladies, this is no laughing matter.

ALLEGRA. Who's joking?

JAMES. *(To HOLLISTER.)* You had better explain.

HOLLISTER. Yes, sir. You see, I have grown very fond of Miss Beatrice over the years. The reason I never married is because I love her deeply, though I could never tell her so, of course. It wouldn't be proper.

BEATRICE. *(Touching HOLLISTER's arm.)* Hollister ... how sweet ....

HOLLISTER. *(Taking her hand in both of his.)* I was terrified Mr. Worthington would send you away, as were you. When the lights went out and you stepped past me in the dark to go to the table ....

JAMES. *(Cutting in.)* How did you know that?

HOLLISTER. I smelled her perfume — primrose. Then I heard the knife clatter as Miss Beatrice picked it up. I feared she intended to use it to stab her brother. I couldn't let that happen, so I felt for her hand and took the weapon from her.

JAMES. And stabbed the man yourself?

HOLLISTER. I hadn't intended to, but he fell back against me, and the knife ... I don't expect you to believe it was an accident, but ....

BEATRICE. *(Cutting in.)* Oh, Hollister, I wasn't going to kill Edward! He was my little bubba! I thought the knife was pretty ... it had such a nice, shiny blade ... so while no one could see, I was going to hide it ... I like to hide away lovely things ....

HOLLISTER. I understand, Miss Beatrice. Forgive me for mis-judging you. *(To JAMES.)* It appears I made an unfortunate mistake, sir. I am prepared to do penance for the deed.

INA. You've been a real gentleman's gentleman, Hollister ... well, up until you killed yours, of course.

HOLLISTER. Thank you, Ina. I trust you and Mrs. Vickers and Edith will continue to look after Miss Beatrice? I fear I shall not be returning.

INA. You bet, we will!

MRS. VICKERS. *(Overlapping.)* Don't you worry about that.

EDITH. *(Overlapping.)* We'll take care of her.

JAMES. Hollister. *(HOLLISTER holds out his hands. JAMES*

puts the cuffs on his wrists.) Let's go to the parlor. I need to give headquarters a call.
HOLLISTER. As you wish, sir.

(JAMES takes his arm and they start UL.)

JAMES. The rest of you remain here. Since you witnessed Hollister's confession, I'll need to take your statements later.

(He nods to HOLLISTER. They exit UL.)

BEATRICE. The dear, dear man ....

(DEBRA rises and crosses to her.)

DEBRA. Don't worry, Aunt Bea, we'll get a good lawyer to represent him. Come sit.

(They cross back to the sofa and sit.)

ALLEGRA. A good lawyer? I'd like to know how you plan to pay for one. I appreciate Hollister for getting rid of the old ogre, but I don't intend to spend a fortune to defend him.
DEBRA. You're a cruel, greedy woman, Allegra!
JUSTINE. And those are her better qualities.
ALLEGRA. *(Rising; she will move about at will.)* Needless to say, you and your brat won't be getting any more handouts, either. And as for Beatrice, I'm afraid Hollister's efforts were in vain. A rest home is where she belongs, and I intend to send her to one ... the cheapest one I can find.
BEATRICE. Oh, my ....
DEBRA. You wouldn't!
TONY. I know Sis — yes, she would, and so would I.
PEGGY SUE. Louse.
EDITH. You're horrible! Oh, Mrs. Vickers, you were right! Tony is a terrible man!
MRS. VICKERS. I figured you'd realize that, sooner or later. I'm

just glad it's sooner.

ALLEGRA. While I'm cleaning house, Roy, I expect your resignation tomorrow. From what we've all learned tonight, your business methods leave a lot to be desired.

ROY. But I explained ...!

CONNIE. *(Overlapping.)* Allegra, Roy wouldn't ....

ALLEGRA. *(Cutting in.)* Oh, I don't blame you for what you did.... I just don't want you doing it with my money.

LAWRENCE. *(Rising.)* But it's not your money, and never will be.

ALLEGRA. What!?!

(Everyone reacts.)

LAWRENCE. Edward left a will. I'll schedule a formal reading later, but I'll tell you the gist of it now. He left everything to his daughter, Debra, with two provisions: first, that should she marry, she will retain her maiden name, and that if she should produce a son, she will name him Edward the fourth after him.

DEBRA. I don't have any problem with that.

LAWRENCE. He also stipulated that you are to provide for his sister, Beatrice's, care for the rest of her life.

DEBRA. I would have done that gladly anyway. *(She hugs BEATRICE.)* Gee, Mom, I guess Father really did care something about me.

JUSTINE. What do you know? The old boy had a heart after all.

(JAMES and HOLLISTER enter and stand UL. ALLEGRA doesn't notice them.)

ALLEGRA. *(Furious.)* What about me!?! He owes me something, too! I gave him the best years of my life!

PEGGY SUE. From what he told me, that's not saying a lot.

ALLEGRA. Oh, shut up! Well, Lawrence, what did Edward leave me?

LAWRENCE. Your Louis Viton luggage and as many of your clothes as you can pack into them. Period.

(He sits. ALLEGRA cries out, enraged.)
    ALLEGRA. Luggage! You mean I killed the old tightwad for nothing!?!

(Everyone reacts.)

    TONY. *(Jumping to his feet.)* Sis!
    ALLEGRA. *(Pacing furiously DS, exploding in anger.)* I, too, heard the knife clatter when Beatrice picked it up, and saw it glimmer faintly! I knew someone behind him was holding it! I wasn't sure that whoever held it had the guts to kill him, so I gave Edward a shove backward! Yes, I helped skewer the man, and I'm glad I did it!
    JAMES. Very interesting. *(He unlocks HOLLISTER's handcuffs.)* It seems I'm going to have another use for these, Hollister.
    HOLLISTER. I am happy to return them, sir.
    TONY. *(Rushing to ALLEGRA who is DR by this point.)* Sis! Don't say anything else!
    JAMES. *(Crossing to them, stepping over the outline.)* That advice is too late, Mr. Blackwell. Apparently when Hollister said Mr. Worthington fell against the knife, he was telling the truth. He isn't the killer, but the woman who pushed her husband onto the blade is. Allegra Worthington, I'm arresting you for the murder of Edward Worthington the third.

(He puts the cuffs on her wrists.)

    ALLEGRA. *(Still hysterical.)* Take me away! I don't care! Just take me out of this house!
    JAMES. It's a pleasure. My men are on the way in a squad car. We can wait for them out front.

*(He leads her toward the archway, stepping over the outline. ALLE-
    GRA pauses, turns back, then grinds her shoe in the outline.)*

    ALLEGRA. Good riddance!

(JAMES leads her through the archway and they exit UR. We hear the

door open and close.)
JUSTINE. I don't believe it! Somebody finally used the front door!

(BEATRICE rises and crosses to HOLLISTER UL. TONY slumps dejectedly onto Allegra's chair DS of the table SR.)

BEATRICE. Hollister ... you sweet man. Why didn't you tell me how you felt ages ago?
HOLLISTER. It wouldn't have been the correct thing to do, Miss Beatrice.
BEATRICE. Piffle! We'll discuss the subject later ... in private.

(She slips her hand into his.)

HOLLISTER. Yes, madam.

(His usually stern features dissolve into a warm smile.)

DEBRA. *(Rising and moving at will.)* Hollister, perhaps it would help solve your problem if you were no longer Aunt Bea's butler. I think it's time you retired, with a very generous pension. And you are welcome to continue living in Worthington Manor as long as you like.
HOLLISTER. *(Touched; softly.)* Oh, Miss Debra ....
DEBRA. Mrs. Vickers, Ina, Edith, you are a part of our family. You've showed me more love than poor Father was ever able to. I hope none of you ever leave.

(They murmur quiet assurances they care for her too.)

ROY. Uh ... Debra ... about my job ...?
DEBRA. No one can deny you've invested Father's money brilliantly, Roy, but I'm not sure I approve of all your methods. You may continue to act as financial advisor for Worthington Enterprises, but I expect you to meet with me every Friday afternoon to go over the books. If I find anything irregular ....
ROY. You won't! The figures will look like textbook examples! I

swear!

DEBRA. Fine.

CONNIE. Does that mean you still have your job?

ROY. Yes, Connie.

CONNIE. Oh, good! Wal-Mart is having a fall blow-out sale tomorrow! I'll be there when the doors open!

ROY. Whatever you say.

(Unconsciously, he scratches his arm. Is he developing hives?)

LAWRENCE. If you are taking over the management of the company, Debra, you'll need a good lawyer more than ever.

DEBRA. Don't worry, Lawrence, I'm sure between us, Mom and I will be able to find one. We'll make sure it's a lawyer who doesn't betray his client's confidence.

LAWRENCE. You mean I'm fired?

JUSTINE. Like a gas grill on the Fourth of July, baby! And Lawrence, you can tell that writer fella, Jamison, that's he's wasting his time if he intends to finish that book. If there's going to be a biography published about Edward, I'm the one who should write it. I think it's safe to say a bio by his first wife who was there when he was murdered will knock any other writer's version right off the bookstore shelves.

DEBRA. Mom, are you really ...?

JUSTINE. I am, if you'll help. Your father was a tyrant, but he was my tyrant, and I'll tell it like it is. I'm sure if I try hard enough, I can find a few good things to say about him. What do you think?

DEBRA. I think it's a great idea. He did pay you alimony when he didn't have to, and he provided for me and Aunt Bea.

PEGGY SUE. If you need somebody to take shorthand and type it up, I'm a darn good secretary.

DEBRA. Mom?

JUSTINE. Oh, why not? You were taking Edward away from Allegra, not me, so you gave her a taste of her own medicine. I guess I owe you something for that.

DEBRA. You can stay on board, Peggy Sue.

PEGGY SUE. Thanks a whole bunch. To tell you the truth, I'm

glad I'm going to be working for women for a change. Maybe now all the bruises I got where I keep getting pinched will clear up.

TONY. I guess that covers everyone but me. Where do I stand?

DEBRA. Out in the cold, Tony. Edith summed you up perfectly — you're a terrible man. If I see you around here after tonight, I'll sic the dogs on you.

TONY. You don't own any dogs.

DEBRA. I'll buy some. *(Police sirens are heard faintly in the distance.)* Apparently Lt. McMillan's men are arriving. Allegra is going to be behind bars for a long, long time.

JUSTINE. She has one thing going for her, though.

DEBRA. What's that, Mom?

JUSTINE. She's always looked great in stripes.

(Blackout. JAMES and ALLEGRA, without the handcuffs, enter at the French doors. JAMES/EDWARD/WALTER lies down in the tape outline on the floor CS. The others recreate the tableau they held at the end of Act I when the lights came on and they discovered Edward's body. The lights come up on this tableau. The actors will break their freeze in turn and bow to the audience with JAMES/EDWARD/WALTER being the last to do so.)

WALTER. There you have it, ladies and gentlemen, a murder deconstructed and played out for your enjoyment and edification. Speaking for the playwright — I am his alter-ego, you recall — I hope you had a good time. All of us did. Goodnight.

(The cast takes a company bow or two. Blackout and ... curtain)

Property List

Pre-set:
Pillows - on sofa
Dish of mints - on table SR
Vase - on table UL

Between Prologue & Act I Scene 1:
Strike coffee cup

Between Act I, Scenes 1& 2:
Strike trays of hors d'oeuvres
Strike tray & wine glasses
Beatrice removes dish from pocket

Between Acts I & II
Put ink on fingertips — cast
Tape outline on floor
Strike play money, coffee cup, tea cup, birthday cake, tray of items,
    champagne bucket & bottle, tray & champagne glasses

Personal:
Cup/coffee – Tony
Legal pad & pen - Walter
(2) tray/hors d'oeuvres (some with olive slices) - Edith
Napkin - Beatrice
Gift (necktie) - Tony
Gift (pen & pencil set) - Allegra
Gift (sweater) - Connie
Gift (huge) - Peggy Sue
(2) tray/wine glasses/wine - Edith
Briefcase/small gift & sealed envelope of blank pages - Lawrence
Gift - Debra
Eye glasses - Edward
Monopoly money - Connie
Cup/coffee - Tony *(repeat of prologue)*
Birthday cake - Ina

Tray/saucers, forks, napkins, cake server, knife, knife handle hidden
    under napkins - Edith
Blood capsule - Edward
Cup/tea - Beatrice
Bucket/champagne - Ina
Tray/champagne glasses/champagne - Edith
Pad & pen - James
Cell phone - James
Vase - Beatrice
Flowers - Debra
Blood - Tony
Toilet paper - Tony
Handkerchief - Roy
(2) trays/hors d'oeuvres - Ina, Edith
Handcuffs & key - James

Production Notes

Costumes:

Walter is dressed in casual clothes—cotton pants and sport shirt or sweatshirt. Tony, Roy, Lawrence, Hollister and Edward wear tuxedos. Allegra, Justine, Debra, Beatrice, Connie and Peggy Sue wear attractive gowns or cocktail dresses. Justine and Debra also need coats. Mrs. Vickers wears a plain, dark dress. Edith wears a typical maid's uniform -- black dress, white apron and cap. Ina wears a cook's uniform—white dress and long apron. James wears an open trench coat over a suit and tie, and a fedora hat.

Triple Role:

The actor who plays Walter, Edward and James should create different personalities for each man, of course. Walter is easy-going and friendly; Edward is cold and controlling; James is serious about his job, but has an underlying sense of humor.

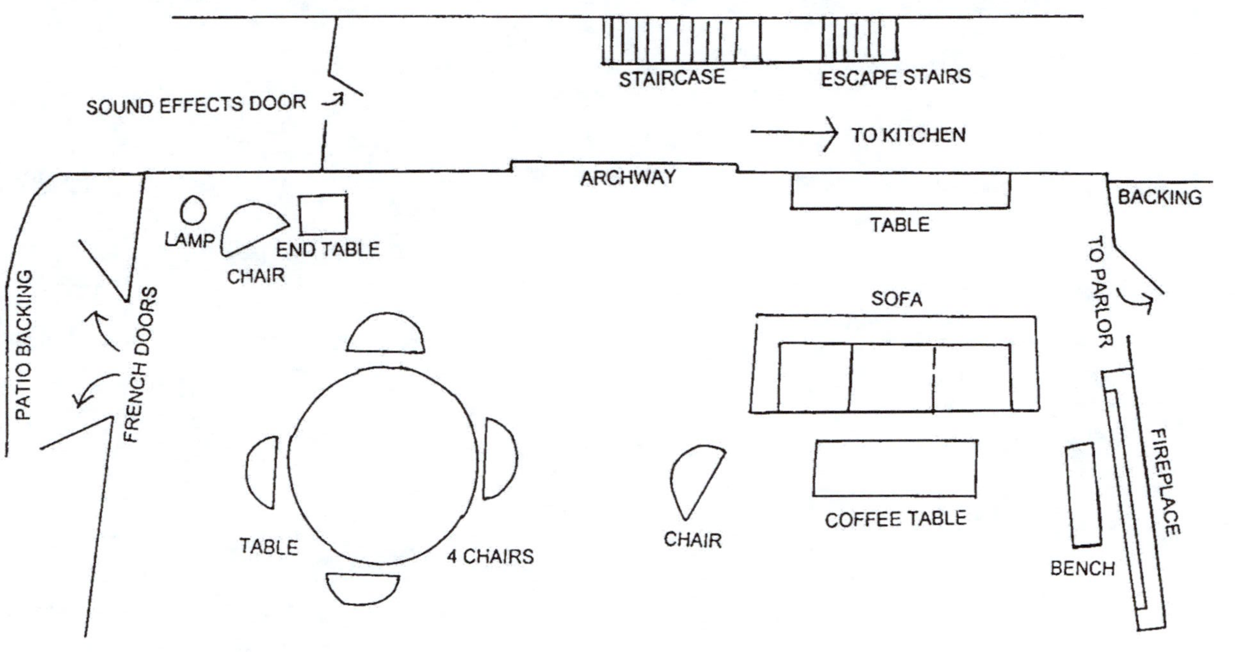

THE PLOT, LIKE GRAVY, THICKENS

www.ingramcontent.com/pod-product-compliance
Lightning Source LLC
Chambersburg PA
CBHW070353120726
47909CB00008B/2832